Good

"I can blanket this horse," Clint said sharply.

Cait glanced up at him, held his gaze. "You can certainly *ride* him," she said sincerely. "You two looked like poetry out there."

Her words stunned him. So did the pleasure that ran through him.

"Compliments don't excuse you sneaking up on me," he muttered.

She grinned. "Don't worry, Clint," she said. "I won't tell your secret."

"Tell whatever you want," he snapped.

She chuckled and handed him the buckle strap. "So you're not vulnerable to blackmail?"

He snorted. "As if you'd need blackmail, Cait. I'm thinking a bulldozer's more your style."

She straightened suddenly, at the very same time he did, and smiled at him across the horse.

He couldn't keep from watching her smile and noticing the sparkle in her dark eyes. In fact, he couldn't mov̶e̶ ̶.̶.̶.̶ ̶s̶u̶d̶d̶e̶n̶l̶y̶ all he could do was loo̶k̶

Books by Gena Dalton

Love Inspired

Stranger at the Crossroads #174
Midnight Faith #189

GENA DALTON

wanted to be a professional writer from the time she learned to read at the age of four. However, she became a secondary school teacher and then a college professor/dean of women instead, and began to write only after she was married and became a stay-at-home mother. She entered an essay contest, which resulted in a newspaper publication that gave her confidence she could achieve her lifelong dream of becoming a "real writer."

Gena lives in Oklahoma with her husband of twenty-four years. Now that their son is grown, their only companions are two dogs, two house cats, one barn cat and one cat who belongs to the neighbors but won't go home.

She loves to hear from readers. She can be reached c/o Steeple Hill Books, 300 East 42nd Street, 6th floor, New York, NY 10017.

Midnight Faith
Gena Dalton

♥ *Love Inspired*®

Published by Steeple Hill Books™

STEEPLE HILL BOOKS

Steeple
Hill™

ISBN 0-373-87196-1

MIDNIGHT FAITH

Copyright © 2002 by Genell Dellin

Visit us at www.steeplehill.com

Printed in U.S.A.

He went on to say, "What is the kingdom of God like? What shall I compare it with? It is like a mustard seed, which a man took and threw into his garden; it grew and became a tree, and the birds of the air sheltered in its branches."

—*Luke* 13:18-19

For my sisters,
Linda and Bonnie

Chapter One

Something was definitely wrong when a man had to sneak around before daylight to ride a horse on his own place.

It added to his pleasure, though. Clint whistled a tune, very softly, as he led the tall black colt out of the barn toward the indoor arena, its hooves echoing out into the frosty air until they left the asphalt for the gravel. Then the sound lessened to a muted, homey plop.

His guess would be that sitting in the saddle on this lanky rascal would be anything but homey, though. His heartbeat sped up. This colt might be the biggest challenge of all the two-year-olds on the ranch this year.

The black snorted, shook his head and spooked at the kitten that came tumbling out of the tack room ahead of its brother. Then he kicked up behind when Clint tied him.

"Now, now," Clint said, grinning, "give me a chance to take a seat before you get to bucking, all right?"

He gave the colt a pat on the neck—which bothered him so much he pinned his ears—and went to get the saddle. The tune he kept whistling was "Two-Step around the Christmas Tree," which he couldn't get out of his head and which irritated him to no end. If it was left up to him, they'd just skip Christmas this year here on the Rocking M.

Clint slapped that thought right out of his head with his usual skill. Right now would be the best time of his Christmas Eve and he was going to enjoy it without thinking ahead. Or back.

It added a little spice to life, having a secret vice, and it amused him every day. So far, neither of the trainer's assistants had stepped down off a colt and wondered aloud if somebody else had already ridden him.

Mainly because the idea was inconceivable. The least-skilled horsemen on the trainer's staff, the assistants to the assistant, started the colts because nobody else wanted that hard, dangerous job. They were young and their bodies could take it.

Clint grinned again. It'd blow everybody's minds, for sure, to know that the ranch's owner was doing that work, and he would surely get a kick out of telling them. He couldn't, though, because it would insult the hands whose duty it was, implying that they weren't doing their jobs. It would also insult the trainers who supervised those hands, and they'd accuse him of messing up their training programs for these horses.

More to the point, they'd all probably leave the Rocking M and go somewhere else because Clint had not respected their territory. He wouldn't take that chance—winning trainers who brought attention and celebrity to the ranch were hard to find.

His grin faded. Always, always and forever, he had to do what was good for the ranch.

Sometimes he felt he *was* the ranch and not a person anymore.

The colt stood, although his ears were still pinned. He let Clint ease the saddle and pad onto him and cinch him up before he kicked out again. Clint's heart made a triple beat. This one would be the liveliest of the bunch.

He'd sensed that all along, which was why he'd left him for last, he supposed. If the black dumped him and he broke a bone, he would already have had the excitement of riding the others.

He untied the colt and led him into the indoor arena, closed the gate behind them and reached over the fence for a bridle hanging on the rack. The black stood quietly while he exchanged it for the halter, then walked just as quietly as he led him farther into the pen.

After arranging the reins, Clint took hold of the horn and the cantle and lifted his weight onto the saddle, hanging off the side of the horse. No problem. The black didn't even move—forward, back or sideways.

Clint stepped up into the saddle.

Both feet set in the stirrups, he shifted carefully back and forth. Nothing.

He settled his weight into the depth of the seat. No movement from the young horse. Maybe he'd been entirely wrong about him.

Clint made himself take in a deep breath and then wait, letting it out slowly. The whole, quiet, darkest-before-dawn world waited with him to see what this colt would do.

All he did was look around. Clint followed his gaze. The lighted arena made the patch of night that showed through the top half of the south door as black as the horse.

The glass wall to the customers' lounge was a dark blank. This morning there were no owners sitting in front of the fireplace talking, getting drinks from the refrigerators, or swiveling in the leather easy chairs to watch the wide-screen TV and their horse being ridden at the same time. No one at all intruding into Clint's own private world.

The black stared at the glass for so long that Clint realized he was looking at his own reflection. He probably thought it was another horse.

"You're not gonna spook at your own shadow, are you now, Midnight?"

That was the last coherent thought he had. The colt dropped his head and gave a mighty pitch so fast Clint hadn't even sensed him thinking about it. His hat flew off, the seat of his pants separated from the saddle, he grabbed for his balance, and from then on, everything he did was on instinct.

His legs clamped the colt's sides and one hand tangled in the mane as his center of gravity shifted, but he still would have gone over and off if Midnight hadn't raised his head right then and caught Clint along his neck. The steady, waiting world was long gone as fast as if it had never been, turned upside down and spun sideways.

All he knew was blurs of fence and dirt and the black's long mane, whipping around. It caught him across the face once, twice, as the jarring landings shook him looser. Finally, by a superhuman effort, using the momentum of the next jump, he fought his way back into the saddle. His balance came back, too. Sort of.

Everything turned to motion and speed, into flying jumps and hard, punishing landings. All he could do was try to keep breath in his body while he tried even harder not to come loose again.

At last, after an eternity of uncertainty, he could feel the rhythm, he could anticipate the force, he could judge how much and which way to respond, and the thrill of staying on began to pound into his blood. He and Midnight traveled across the arena and back to the other side molded together into one plunging, rising, falling animal.

Eventually they stretched out into a run. The wind they created blew the colt's mane back toward Clint and he glanced toward the glass wall to see the wild picture the black horse made as he flew around the arena.

He had this one now. But only this one ride. It'd be a long time before he'd expect the big black colt not to buck, at least a little.

Maybe he ought to ride him every morning instead of rotating through all the others. This was a horse after his own restless heart.

The truth was that this secret fun was the only reason he was glad to get up in the morning. Everything else seemed to be work. Duty. Responsibility. All his and only his.

They rounded the southwest corner and started down the straightaway.

Clint glimpsed somebody standing at the rail. His gut tensed. He looked again.

But he'd known who it was from that first, fast flash in the corner of his eye. That mass of black curly hair catching the arena lights was unmistakable. That and her bold stance.

He sat back and murmured to the colt.

"Whoa. Whoa, now, Midnight."

Midnight didn't whoa, but he did slow down.

By some miracle of Clint's determination, or maybe because the colt was actually tiring at last, he rode him to a stop in front of her with a tolerable show of control.

Her straight look hadn't changed a bit. He met it with one of his own.

"Caitlin O'Doyle."

Her name came off his lips sounding like a challenge.

She challenged him right back, as always.

"It's McMahan."

Instead of ignoring her and riding on, as he should've done, he fell into fussing with her as naturally as breathing.

"I thought you might've changed it back by now."

"No," she said, and propped one booted foot on the bottom rail as she folded her long, graceful arms along the top one. "It's still McMahan...just like yours. Clint."

Her crisp northern accent might've softened a little, but nothing else about her had changed one whit. She still held herself as if she owned Texas for as far as she could see, and all the cattle in it. That high, straight-bridged nose of hers still gave her that haughty look and her tall, voluptuous shape still begged for a man's hands.

Or maybe it was the other way around. Caitlin O'Doyle McMahan never begged. She never even bent.

If she had bent enough to go to Mexico with John, his brother would be alive today. And he, Clint, would still have one of his brothers, at least, by his side every day.

"Why don't you get a life, Cait? You ought to be back in Chicago by now."

Her big dark eyes flashed.

"I'd never presume to tell *you* to get a life, Clint."

She glanced around the empty arena.

"But then, maybe that's because you already have one. Riding colts alone in the middle of the night must be a thrill a minute."

Hot fury sliced at his gut. Was it because she still attracted him so much, even when she was making fun of him? Even when he knew she hadn't done right by John?

The black shifted beneath him and tried to drop his head, but Clint wouldn't let him. He gave Cait a hard stare while the horse stepped to the left, then back to the right.

"You appear to be out alone in the middle of the night, yourself, Cait."

"I got a late start from Tulsa."

"They celebrate Christmas in Tulsa, too, last I heard."

Her eyes, black as her hair, sparked with fire.

"Your mother invited me, Clint. This is her ranch. Bobbie Ann can invite anyone she wants for Christmas."

"It's my ranch, too."

"And that is exactly the reason I'm interrupting your night ride," she said, looking at his horse instead of him as the black danced sideways. "To ask you, the co-owner and general manager, where I should unload my horses."

She stared at the colt for a minute, then met Clint's gaze again. He clenched his jaw so hard he could hardly speak. One reason Cait had always irritated him so was that she had no end of nerve.

"Your horses," he repeated flatly.

"Yes."

"How many head?"

"Seven."

What in the name of good sense was she doing dragging seven head of horses in here?

"I know you don't want to miss any of the McMahan festivities," he said sarcastically, "but it's early yet. So why don't we do it this way? You take a run on over to Roy's and unload his horses and we'll hold up on the eggnog until you get back. How's that?"

"These aren't Roy's horses."

He stared at her, trying to figure out what she was up to and steady the colt at the same time. All he needed now was to fool around and let the black throw him right in front of her.

"Then whose are they?"

"Mine."

He stared at her some more. She was so full of life and so full of confidence. Not once did she smile or try to charm him into giving permission, as another woman might have done.

"Did Bobbie Ann invite you for Christmas or for the rest of your life?"

"Roy's not going to let an assistant trainer keep any personal horses over there, much less seven head," she said, so reasonably that he wanted to punch something. "You know that."

His blood ran cold, then hot, with anger.

"Are you telling me that you just drove to Tulsa and bought seven head of horses that you're fixing to keep here? On the Rocking M?"

He bit his tongue to hold back the rest of the words that leapt to it. He ought to go ahead and tell her to haul them on out of here, but he didn't. Never had he ever known anyone, man or woman, who had this much sand.

She looked up at him with an expression he couldn't quite read.

"Yes."

"How long do you want to leave 'em?"

She shrugged her beautifully square shoulders, tilted her head to the side and he saw once again what every man always saw: Caitlin McMahan wasn't really what you'd call beautiful, but she was one magnificent woman. Already. And she was barely past being a girl.

"I'll be straight with you, Clint," she said, unnecessarily. "I want to leave 'em indefinitely. I told Bobbie Ann not to say anything because I wanted to tell you myself."

Tell you. Not ask you. That was Cait.

He stood in the stirrup and stepped down off the black. Whatever she was up to, he'd better give it his full attention. This could affect him for a long time to come.

Without another word he led the colt toward the gate. Sure enough, Cait met him there. She walked at the colt's other shoulder as they headed for the saddling bay.

"I'm starting a riding school," she said.

That was Cait, again. Not "wanting to" or "planning to," but doing it. She wasn't asking permission, either.

"On the Rocking M," he said.

His tongue was thickening with fury. His blood thundered with it. She'd be hanging around, here in plain sight, all the time.

She read his mind.

"I'll only be here a couple of hours in the evenings," she said. "I won't interfere with your trainers or anybody else using your facilities."

He tied the colt and began uncinching the saddle. He paused to glare at her.

"They have amateurs that come to ride in the evenings," he snapped.

Why'd she have to get this insane idea in the first place? Why couldn't she just stay away from the Rocking M the way she'd been doing?

"I know," she said. "But I'll only be here in the late afternoons and I'll use the old outdoor pen."

"Give me a break, Cait," he interrupted. "Ask my permission, at least."

She flashed those eyes at him again.

"I don't have to, Clint," she said. "I have every right to be here."

"Don't start telling me you inherited part of this ranch from John," he said harshly. "It's bad enough you're spending his blood money."

She stiffened.

"You know he'd still be alive if you'd gone with him," he blurted. "With his wife there to protect, he'd never have taken any chances."

Cait stepped right up and got in his face.

"Watch your mouth," she growled, her eyes bright with fury. And hurt. Maybe even with tears. Maybe tears of guilt.

Even if she did feel guilty, shame stabbed through him. He had crossed a grave line here and he wasn't one to do that.

"Sorry," he muttered.

He turned his back on her, unwrapped the latigo, took the saddle and pad off, and strode toward the tack room, searching his mind frantically for a way to get rid of her. Bobbie Ann had already heard about this, and, knowing her, she'd approved the idea.

She would welcome Cait's presence every day. She would say it reminded her of how happy John had been in his marriage to Cait.

And he had been, poor sucker. Nobody had ever been able to figure out why the striking, bold nineteen-year-old girl from up north who'd come to Texas to be Roy Bassett's assistant trainer had ever agreed to marry quiet, thoughtful, unexciting John McMahan. It had to be the name, the ranch, the money.

Wasn't that true of 90 percent of the women who chased after any of the McMahan brothers?

Cait O'Doyle could've had any man in Texas if

she'd so much as crooked her finger. Any one of those men would have been a better match for her than John.

Why, even *he* would've been a better match for a girl with her spirit.

He took as long as he could to put the saddle on the wall and the steaming pad to dry on the rack. That reminded him that the colt had worked up a sweat and he needed to get him back to the stall.

What was he doing, letting Caitlin's appearance and then her announcement unsettle him? This was ridiculous. He could handle her and her half-baked ideas.

Quickly he crossed the hallway again and went into the open bay. Cait was rubbing the colt down.

"I want to get him back and get him blanketed," he said.

"Right," she said in a sensible tone, and stepped away to drop the rubber currycomb into the tray that topped the roll-around cart.

"Thanks," he said stupidly, before he thought.

Out of guilt? Or in an effort to prove he did have some manners, after all? What was the matter with him, giving her any shred of encouragement to do *anything* around here?

For answer, she looked over her shoulder and smiled at him. His pulse raced.

Maybe she wasn't beautiful, but her smile certainly was. At every horse show some guy said something about her smile. Or just about her, period.

Well, about her looks or her horsemanship or

what a good hand she was. Very few people knew anything about *her*.

He avoided looking at her again, went to the colt's head and untied him, started to lead him away. He needed a chance to think. Surely he could figure out a way to keep her from hanging around the Rocking M all the time.

But he could hear her footsteps following him down the gravel incline and across the paved street to the barn.

"I surely do hate to bother you, Clint," she said dryly, "but I'd like to get unloaded and make it to the house in time for some of Bobbie Ann's hot biscuits."

Well, there was no hope for it. Bobbie Ann would have his hide if he caused a big fuss and ruined Christmas Eve, so he might as well find a temporary spot for Cait's horses.

"The quarantine barn's empty," he said, throwing the words at her over his shoulder.

"Fine. Thanks."

But she didn't turn and start back to her truck. A quick glance from the corner of his eye told him that.

He moved faster, tried to walk away from her into the long, limestone barn, but she stayed right with him the whole way. He ignored her, led the colt to his stall and took the blanket from the rack on the door.

Cait walked around them and went to the black's

head, grasped the lead right under his chin to hold him. Clint refused to turn loose of the rope.

"You're in a hurry," he growled. "Go on."

"Not that big a hurry," she said absently, stepping back to look the colt over as if he were the only thing in the barn.

Clint clenched his teeth. Wasn't that just like a woman? Just like *Cait*—first she's in a fit to be gone and the next minute you can't run her off with a stick.

He gathered the blanket and went to slip it over the colt's head.

"I've *got* him," he said sharply.

"So have I," she said, laughing a little as she helped manage the blanket.

"Very funny," he said sarcastically.

She was, without a doubt, the stubbornest woman he'd ever met.

Their hands brushed together as they brought the big blanket over the colt's tossing head. Cait's bare fingers were surprisingly warm in this frosty weather—warm enough to send a twinge of heat through him.

The black stepped sideways. Cait moved with the colt, keeping parallel with Clint to spread the blanket. He set his jaw. Why didn't she just go on about her business and get out of his?

Why didn't she go away, so he couldn't catch even one faint drift of her citrusy scent?

"I can blanket this horse," he said sharply.

She glanced up at him, held his gaze.

"You can certainly *ride* him," she said sincerely. "You two looked like poetry out there."

That stunned him. So did the pleasure that ran through him with her words.

"Compliments don't excuse you sneaking up on me," he muttered.

She grinned before she leaned over to reach under the colt's belly to hand him the strap to buckle.

"Don't worry, Clint," she said. "I won't tell your secret."

"Tell whatever you want," he snapped.

She chuckled as she handed him the other strap.

"So you're not vulnerable to blackmail, huh, Clint?"

He snorted. "As if you'd *need* blackmail, huh, Cait? I'm thinking a bulldozer's more your style."

She straightened suddenly, at the very same time he did, and smiled at him across the horse.

"Aw, come on. It's Christmas. Let's not fight."

He couldn't keep from watching that smile. He couldn't keep from noticing the sparkle in her dark eyes.

To tell the truth, he couldn't move a muscle. Suddenly all he wanted was to look at Cait.

"Hey, Clint, Christmas Eve gift," she said.

The ancient greeting handed down from his Appalachian ancestors startled him once more. The magic phrase that claimed the other person's first gift filled him with sudden memories of playing this game with his brothers. Then it filled him with anger and regret. She had no business even saying it—it sounded strange in her northern accent.

"Always one for a little family tradition, huh, Cait?"

Quick, deep hurt showed in her big dark eyes. It wiped her smile away.

Guilt tugged at him. He was never one to be deliberately cruel and he'd spoken before he thought. Cait was practically an orphan—she had no family traditions of her own.

She was tough, though, this Irish girl from Chicago. A little hurt would never damage her confidence.

"Yes. Ever since I fell in love with your brother I've been into the traditions of *this* family."

She gave him that straight look of hers that dared him to contradict her.

"I'm a McMahan, too, Clint, whether you like it or not."

He *didn't* like it, but there wasn't a blessed thing he could do about it.

From the instant she got back into her truck and turned the key in the ignition, Cait wouldn't let herself think beyond the moment at hand. Not one second beyond it.

The night was beginning to lighten from true black to a hint of gray as she put the gearshift into Reverse and backed away from the indoor arena. While she pulled out into the paved street and drove past the west end of the barn, she watched the sky in her rearview mirror, waiting for the first glow of pink to prove that the day truly was coming.

Her eyes burned with fatigue and so did her heart, but she wasn't going to think about that now. Not right now. She was unloading her new horses into their new home and after that she'd think about whatever was next.

The security lights scattered over the ranch were still bright against the darkness, and when she'd reached the barn farthest from the other buildings she parked under the light beside its door. Just get them out and comfortably settled, that was all she had to do. Throw them their alfalfa and get them some water.

Suddenly even that seemed like too much to contemplate. Her limbs felt too shaky to do anything.

Cait set her brake and turned on the lights inside the trailer. She'd driven longer trips than this with no more frequent stops than she'd made tonight. She'd hauled Roy's horses all the way to Ohio to the Quarter Horse Congress, nearly twenty-four hours with no relief driver and no sleep.

Exhaustion wasn't her problem.

What *was* the problem?

She snapped her mind away from that next logical thought and got out of the truck. Not allowing so much as a pause to reach back inside for her canvas coat, she headed for the trailer. She'd work fast enough to keep warm in just her fleece jacket.

"You are some fine travelers," she said as she opened the narrow door and stepped up inside, "with, perhaps, an exception here and there. Which one of you has been kicking the side?"

The sight of the nice horses, not great, but plenty good, sound horses—*her* horses—strengthened her. For all these years, she'd never legally owned a horse, and now she owned *seven*. Today or tomorrow, Christmas or not, she'd get all the registration paperwork ready to mail. She couldn't wait to see her name on those official papers.

She let down the padded strap across the rear of the short, roan horse and untied his head.

"I only hope I'm not making a big mistake unloading you here," she confided as she backed him out, "but I can't go somewhere else now. If I find another location for my school, Clint will think he ran me off and he'll only be harder to deal with next time."

And there would *be* a next time, because she was not giving up her rights to be on this ranch. For one thing, the rent money she'd pay somewhere else for facilities could be better spent on more horses for more disadvantaged kids and then for an assistant as their numbers grew.

This school was what the Lord had laid upon her heart and this was what she had to do to the very best of her ability. Her memorial to John would be this school, which would have two purposes: to introduce troubled teenagers to horses and to faith in God.

When Clint knew that, he'd change his attitude. At least, he'd change it a little.

So why hadn't she told him that at once?

She tried to puzzle out the answer as she led the roan into the barn and into the first stall, slipped his halter off and then left him, to get some bags of shavings from the trailer. Maybe it was because she wanted him to acknowledge her right to use the ranch. Maybe it was because she wanted him to know that Bobbie Ann had every right to make decisions, too.

Maybe it was because she wanted Clint to accept her as a person and not only because of John.

That was close.

It was because she wanted him to see her as a woman, not as his brother's wife.

Chapter Two

All he had to do was simply not think of Cait as a woman.

Impatiently Clint popped the shine cloth across the toe of his right boot one more time, put that foot to the floor and set his left one up onto the woven-bark footstool. It was stupid that he'd ever even noticed that she *was* a woman, anyhow.

She was his brother's wife—widow or not—for heaven's sake! She was forward and stubborn and she had no tact whatsoever in any situation. He didn't have the slightest interest in her.

Except, of course, as to how her cockeyed *school* was going to impact his ranch operations. He popped the cloth in the air and then pulled it vigorously across his already-shiny left boot.

He snorted. Her staying out of everybody's way and using only the old outdoor pen was nothing but a pipe dream. Just let the temperature go above a hundred, let the wind blow dust in their eyes at forty miles an hour, and Caitlin and her little-rich-girl clients would be cluttering up the indoor arena from one end to the other. They'd turn the whole place upside down and probably drive his trainers so crazy they'd quit.

And that kind of trouble he did not need—especially not now, when he was making so many decisions about the ranch and its future. He absolutely would not lose two top trainers who were winning at all the big shows and bringing attention and dollars to the ranch.

What he *would* do was find a way to get Cait's silly school off this ranch and to another location as soon as humanly possible. He'd talk to Bobbie Ann and start pushing for that just as soon as Christmas was over.

He could see his face in his boot, so he threw the rag back into the wooden box and went to wash his hands before he touched his white shirt. It was time to go downstairs and get on with this poor excuse for a Christmas Eve. Dad, John and Monte all being absent was an unbearable thought, especially for the late-night hot-chocolate family time, and Caitlin's presence was the icing on the cake. As if he didn't have enough to think about!

All he wanted was to get this Christmas over with.

Tonight he would simply look at Caitlin as a sister-in-law, exactly as he did Darcy, Jackson's new wife. That was the one bright spot of the past year—

Jackson's sudden marriage and his gradual rejoining of the human race.

Clint tucked in his shirt, went to the armoire for a belt, selected the saddle-tan one that matched the boots, put a buckle on it and threaded it through the loops of his pants. It would serve Caitlin right, pushy as she was, if he did convince Bobbie Ann that this riding school business was a bad idea. He had a ranch to run, he was responsible for everything that happened on it, he didn't have time to deal with the trouble Caitlin was bound to bring to it and he didn't owe her the time of day.

He hooked the buckle, gave his hair one last, quick swipe with the brush and headed for the door. Well, if he were perfectly honest, he did owe Cait an apology. That crack he'd made about family traditions had been cruel and he hated the sharp pain it had brought to her big dark eyes.

Least said, soonest forgotten, though. No sense in bringing it up and hurting her feelings all over again.

He strode across his room and out into the hallway, glancing toward the guest rooms on that wing. Cait had slept all day, Bobbie Ann had said—not that he'd asked about her—and he'd heard that before breakfast, even, Manuel had asked her for instructions so his crew could feed her horses and take care of them for her.

Poor Manuel. Evidently he was as goofy as all men were about the tall, black-haired, long-legged horsewoman with the million-dollar smile. He'd probably hire a couple more stable hands just to wait on her hand and foot.

He started down the stairs, taking them two at a time.

Manuel had said her horses were good, sound stock but not world-class. Said half of them weren't tall enough to compete in English classes, which was Cait's specialty over at Roy's.

That right there made him wonder what she was really up to. Maybe she was planning a horse-trading business here on his ranch, where all the chores were done efficiently and on schedule and any problems would be taken care of by him and Manuel.

Which, come to think of it, would explain her smiling at him this morning and teasing him and saying let's not fight, when they had never been in the same room in their lives when they didn't fuss and wrangle about something. That must be it.

All Cait wanted from him was free rent at an efficiently run stable.

Even if that were true, though, it didn't excuse him for not helping her unload and get her horses settled. He felt ashamed every time he thought about that—he would've extended the courtesy to anybody else in the world, since none of the hands had come to work yet.

He had never shown anyone such a lack of hospitality.

What was it about Cait that made him behave like a stranger to himself?

What was it about Cait that made him obsess about her every time he saw her?

Cait hardly knew the woman who looked back at her from the mirror.

She wore a skirt, for one thing, a very feminine, clingy, black velvet skirt cut with a bell flare at the below-calf hem, and with it, a white silk blouse that had cost as much as a good work saddle. Never in her entire life had she owned such an expensive garment. She still could not believe she had bought it.

Or that the moment she'd tried it on at that expensive shop in Dallas, she'd thought of Clint. Had imagined Clint seeing her in it.

Tears stung her eyes at her own foolishness, but she forced herself to blink them away and meet her own gaze.

"Face reality," she told her reflection.

She hadn't survived this long without knowing how to do that.

Lifting her chin, she looked it right in the eye: Clint might be attracted to her, too—maybe—but what he also felt for her was scorn.

And she was not accepting any scorn tonight.

Tonight was Christmas Eve. She was invited to a family celebration. Of *her* family.

For the four months of her marriage to John, the two of them had lived on the ranch in a small house about two miles away from headquarters. They had come back from their elopement in time for New

Year's Eve and she'd been in the family for Easter that year, but this was her first Christmas.

Tears stung her eyes. How could she ever have believed it would be a true Christmas without John?

If she had gone with him to Mexico instead of doing her job for Roy, would it have saved him—as Clint believed it would?

Dear Lord, I hope I wasn't the cause of his dying. Please help me know, once again, that I wasn't.

Most of the time she clung to the assurance she'd achieved through hours of prayer after the very first time she'd heard that theory, which was by accidentally overhearing a conversation between Clint and Jackson at John's funeral. Today, though, Clint's accusation had shaken her.

Her heart beat faster. She tightened the combs holding the mass of her hair on top of her head and pulled at the tendrils curling along her neck.

John was gone. Nothing could bring him back. He would not want her to be sad and mourn for him when she should be happy. He would want her to help make his family happy, too.

Deliberately she set her mind to that goal.

It would be a storybook Christmas—family and friends, a huge tree with ornaments that had been in the family for years and years, a festive dinner, gifts, traditions and singing. They would have hot chocolate late, right before they went up to bed. After the old family friends and *their* Christmas guests came and then left after appetizers and drinks and a dance or two, after the family dinner was over and they'd all sat around telling stories and singing carols and after they'd opened one gift apiece. She would be here for all of it because she was one of the family.

Eagerly she turned and went out into the hallway, savoring the spacious, secure feeling of the old stone house around her. Closing the door of her room behind her, she leaned back against it for a moment, just taking in the scents and sounds of the house before she saw anyone else.

This was the most wonderful house she'd ever been in. The center of it was old, a classic, two-story Texas Hill Country farmhouse squarely built of big, rectangular chunks of limestone carved more than a hundred years earlier out of the dusty land itself. It had the typical wooden porches front and back, and wings on either end of the old house, which had been added on fifty years later.

When those wings were built, the once-small oldest rooms in the center had been converted into a couple of huge ones—the great room and the dining room. The part of the kitchen that held the fireplace also had been in the original house. There were nooks and crannies in these rooms and huge rough-cedar posts and beams bearing the weight of the second floor. All the rooms had high ceilings and wide windows and ceiling fans and the solid feel of a home that had its roots deep in the ground.

She looked up and down the hall of this bedroom wing. Old Man Clint, John's grandfather, had believed every bedroom should have the south breeze or the east breeze or both if possible, so this east wing was family bedrooms and guest rooms, while the west one held a pool room, music room, saddle room, library and spaces for Bobbie Ann's sewing and other activities.

But what Cait loved most was not the space—although it amazed her every time she walked through it—it was the old, settled, secure atmosphere created by the worn oak floors, the square Mexican tiles of the kitchen, the leather furniture that had been there since the house was built, the Navajo rugs on the floors and the walls, the wood worn smooth by much use and many hands, the gorgeous Western paintings and sculptures that had gradually come into the house over the years and now looked as if they'd been born there.

This family had not moved out in the night when the rent was due. This family had not splintered into pieces and sent its children to live with the first relatives who would grudgingly take them.

The long, deep nap that had erased her tiredness had left her senses all open and vulnerable. She trembled as she breathed in the cedar smell of the greenery Bobbie Ann had wrapped around the banister railing of the stairs. There was a strong scent of spices, too, because every few feet a bundle of cinnamon sticks and oranges studded with whole nutmegs were tied into the cedar with a big red bow.

A marvelous Christmas that she'd never forget. That's what John had promised her. And that's what he would want her to have.

She started walking down the hall, and passed Clint's room. The door stood ajar, the light was out. He was already downstairs.

Fine. Let him be anywhere he wanted. She didn't have to talk to him. She wasn't accepting any scorn tonight.

Slowly she walked down the stairs, humming along with the song floating up from below. John had said that his sister Delia's band always played for the dancing. Right now, though, it was a lone guitar playing "White Christmas."

Well, there was no chance of snow in the Hill Country tonight, but Cait didn't care. She didn't even need it. In fact, she didn't want it. It would only remind her of the miserable Christmases of her childhood.

Chatter and laughter rose, then, to drown out the guitar and to fill the whole downstairs. The doorbell rang again as Cait reached the first floor. And she could smell chili. Chili and tamales were the McMahan tradition on Christmas Eve.

Company was the other McMahan tradition. There were six or seven families who had all been friends for generations, and they and any Christmas guests of theirs came to the Rocking M for appetizers and drinks before dinner on Christmas Eve. Probably, in the next two hours, at least a hundred people would come and go from this house.

LydaAnn's trilling laugh sounded above the din of greetings called out by a dozen different voices.

Bobbie Ann demanded that all the guests take off their coats and stay awhile.

Christmas had arrived at the Rocking M.

Cait lingered at the bottom of the stairs, kicking out so she could see her new, custom-made-in-Dallas-by-Matteo black boots. Matteo had created the design just for her: red roses and green, twining vines, carved to have layers and layers of petals and stems, plus white butterflies, all of it inlaid and stitched to perfection.

Western boots with the old traditional high, slanted heels and pointed toes. She could have spent less and gotten a great new pair of English riding boots, which she truly needed, but then she wouldn't feel so much like a Texan, would she?

She grinned at her own silliness and started down the hall toward the huge living room full of people. Maybe no one would notice when she came in and she could just wander around and enjoy the tree and not have to make too much small talk.

"Cait! My goodness! What a gorgeous blouse!"

Bobbie Ann was coming out of the living room with her arms full of wraps and jackets of the guests. Cait went to help her.

"And those boots! Oh! I have to see them. Hold up your skirt!"

"It's all your fault, Bobbie Ann," Cait said. "You've been telling me to indulge myself, so I did."

Bobbie Ann's bright blue eyes looked her over from top to toe.

"You done good, girl," she said, with an approving smile. "You look wonderful tonight."

She let Cait take half her load and led the way toward the master suite.

"I bought this blouse, these boots and seven head of horses," Cait said. "Did I indulge myself enough?"

Bobbie Ann gave her husky chuckle.

"No, but it's a start," she said. "I'll take you shopping after Christmas and we'll buy you a wardrobe for spring."

"I don't want any more clothes," Cait said quickly, although the very thought made her yearn to do it. "And I won't have time, anyhow. As soon as I finish working for Roy every day, I'll have to rush over here and protect my school—Clint is furious at the very idea of it."

"Clint needs a distraction," Bobbie Ann said calmly. "He's trying to work himself to death. Anything new is good for him."

They dumped the coats on the bed and Bobbie Ann turned to Cait with open arms.

"Oh, Cait, I'm so glad you're here," she said.

Cait's heart leapt as they hugged. Clint might not want her here, but his mother truly did.

"I'm glad, too," she said. "Thanks for asking me for Christmas, Bobbie Ann."

"Thanks for coming."

Bobbie Ann stepped back and looked up into her eyes.

"I couldn't have borne it if you'd refused my

invitation, Cait," she said. "You're all I have left
of John."

She took Cait's hand and led her toward the festivities then, but Cait's heart had dropped into her
new boots. Was that the only reason Bobbie Ann
wanted her there? Did she not love her for herself
at all?

Clint stood in front of the fireplace talking to Pete
Kirkland—well, listening to him would be more like
it—and wondering how soon he could get away to
circulate among the other guests. Delia's band was
playing, a lot of people were dancing and he needed
to dance with Aunt Faylene because that had been
their own private Christmas Eve ritual since he was
ten years old.

He also needed to be sure he had a good visit
with Larry Matheson, because he was talking about
breeding a couple of his best champion mares to the
Rocking M's new young cutting stallion, Trader
Doc Bar. Larry was nothing if not stylish and a
leader in the industry, and his enthusiastic support
of the stallion could fill the stud's book for next year
and mark him as the up-and-coming best in the business. It was worth far more than any paid advertising
ever could be.

One thing he did not need to do was apologize to
Cait. That would only encourage her to settle in here
with her horses.

He tried to covertly glance at his watch. It already
felt as if this evening had lasted a year.

Fortunately, just when he thought he couldn't stay in one spot any longer, the doorbell rang and he excused himself from Pete to go to answer it. His parents' lifetime friends, the Carmacks, and the twenty-two guests they were having for Christmas this year poured in through the door.

Lorena Carmack laughed as she kissed Clint's cheek.

"They swarmed on us this time," she said. "Aren't you glad this tradition is only bring all your own guests for appetizers and drinks and not for dinner, too?"

"Ma's made enough chili for everybody in Texas," Clint said hospitably. "Y'all should stay."

"Truly spoken like a man," she said. "We can tell you're not the one arranging the place settings, Clint dear."

He ushered them into the already-crowded great room and was in the middle of introductions all around when Bobbie Ann called to him. He looked up…and saw Cait.

All the music and the talk faded away beneath the roaring of his own blood in his head.

Cait *was* beautiful. He had been wrong about that.

He had never seen her in a skirt, and this one fell over her body like a sunrise coming over the land, touching here and there and then sliding away. She was all softness, all creamy skin and white silk and black velvet. She didn't seem like Cait at all.

She seemed like a stranger.

Except for her unmistakable presence, the way

she held herself and the way she moved that drew the eye of everyone in the room. She still had that distinctive, long-strided walk that said, *I know where I'm going and nobody'd better get in my way.*

The eternal challenge of her was the same. Except for an added one—the tumbled mass of black curls piled high on top of her head made a man want to take out the pins and run his hands through her hair.

Her eyes looked like black velvet—like her skirt.

Finally they rested on him. Just for an instant.

"Cait, honey, you know the Carmacks, don't you?" Bobbie Ann said, and she and Lorena began the introductions all over again.

Cait spoke to everyone in the group except him. No one else noticed. Two of the young men in the group—he thought they were Carmack grandsons—monopolized her as soon as they could.

And then she was gone, drifting away with those boys after a pat on the arm from Bobbie Ann, who was shepherding the Carmack group toward the tables full of food.

Clint just stood there for a long minute, looking after her. Then, mercifully, Aunt Faylene came to claim him.

It was the novelty of it, he decided as he danced with Faylene. Simple novelty was the reason she was getting so much attention from everyone.

Why, he, himself couldn't help but watch Cait in spite of a firm resolution not to give her so much as a glance more than the cool one she'd given him.

No one at the party had ever seen her in a dress

before. Few of them, if any, had ever seen her at a social function.

It was the men, as always, who were most fascinated.

Those two young Carmack kids were sticking with her, but several others had joined them, vying for her attention to their jokes and stories. Clint set his jaw and guided Faylene in the opposite direction.

"That Cait's a knockout, isn't she?" his aunt said.

Faylene was nearly as good as Bobbie Ann in reading a man's mind in a New York minute.

"Mmm-hmm."

"Half the men here can't see anything but her and the other half are the old codgers with failing eyesight."

"Mmm-hmm."

His lack of response didn't discourage her one bit.

"She's exotic, that's one reason," she said, "besides being so drop-dead striking in every way. You know what I think makes her so interesting?"

That brought his gaze straight to her sharp blue one, so like his mother's. Faylene indulged herself in one gleam of triumph before she answered the question in his look.

"She's different from other women because she gives no quarter."

He looked at her.

"Like the old Texas Rangers?"

"Exactly."

"She's from Chicago, Faylie."

She ignored his little sally.

"Everything about Cait proclaims it," she said seriously. "The look in her eye, the way she walks, the way she keeps her head in her business all the time. No man can resist a challenge like that."

"Hmpf."

Faylene went right on.

"A man gets one chance with Cait," she said. "One."

A strange, sharp feeling, like a warning, pierced him.

"One's enough when he gets the rough side of her tongue."

"Cait's a direct-talking woman," she said. "Y'all are just used to us Texas women sugarcoating everything for you."

"Oh, yeah," he said. "You and Bobbie Ann are the champion sugarcoaters of all time. Steel magnolias is more like it."

"Well, we all have our own styles," his diminutive aunt said sweetly as she looked up at him with a beatific smile. "I, for one, admire a woman who knows what she wants and goes after it. Cait's bound to be a world-class horsewoman and she will be."

"What've you heard about that?"

Maybe Bobbie Ann had talked to her sister about Cait's silly riding school. Maybe he could get some ammunition here to stop it.

But no. Faylene had her own ideas about what was important information.

"You can see she's Black Irish," she said in a reproving tone. "Same as your great-grandpa Murphy—except his eyes were blue. But his hair was midnight-black, just like Cait's."

"So, Jackson must look like him," Clint said, hoping to get her off the subject of Cait.

At least until this endless waltz could be over. Didn't Delia's arms ever get tired of that fiddle?

"You look like your great-grandpa, too," Faylene said. "Tall and black-haired and handsome as can be. Your eyes are different, though—gray as mist instead of blue." She smiled as if he needed comfort. "That's why I used Jackson for an example instead of you." He returned her smile. She was his favorite aunt. "Ooh," she said, "I can't wait until Jackson and Darcy get here! I still could just spank them for having that tiny wedding in the old chapel instead of letting us throw them a great big one. There's five hundred people with their feelings hurt...."

But he couldn't let well enough be. He'd distracted her and now he had to bring her back.

One of the young men appeared to be asking Cait to dance. She was shaking her head and smiling a refusal.

"What does being Black Irish have to do with being a world-class horsewoman?"

Faylene flashed him an incredulous look.

"The Irish have an affinity for horses, you know that. Their emotions and their spirits run deep and they have a strong connection with things unseen."

Clint had to grin at her seriousness.

"The Comanches had a connection with horses," he said.

"Same with them," Faylene said promptly. "Close to the earth—the Comanches and the Irish."

"Giving no quarter, like the Texas Rangers."

"Right!"

She beamed at him.

He laughed and hugged her as Delia's fiddle finally sang out the last note.

"Thanks for the dance and the information, too, Auntie Fay," he said.

"Any time, lovey."

Then the question on his mind came off his tongue of its own accord.

"Why do you think she married John?"

Faylene narrowed her blue eyes and stared up at him.

"Nobody but Cait knows that, sugar," she said. "Whatever I'd say about it would only be speculation."

Clint grinned.

"Well, I wouldn't want to push you into speculation," he said dryly, "since everything else you've told me tonight has been ironclad fact."

"That's exactly right," she said, twinkling at him.

Then she patted him on the arm and hurried off, waving at Jim Prescott. Suddenly she stopped and looked back.

"Sometime she might tell you herself, sweetie," she said.

Oh, sure. Sometime when he and Cait became best buddies.

Immediately, without so much as a glance toward Cait and her admirers, he started looking for Larry. The reason Cait had married John was totally immaterial to him and he had no idea why he'd asked that question out loud.

He didn't even want to know. All he wanted was to make the Rocking M the premier breeding station in the reining-horse industry, and in the meantime come up with new stallions to take over the cutting- and pleasure-horse market, too.

And he also wanted to make some waves with his cattle. Might as well dream big. He was the oldest brother, and he'd always been the most responsible one, so perhaps the whole ranch was meant to fall on his shoulders. Jackson was the next oldest, and he was here on the Rocking M and, in time, might come to share the burden.

Monte, the third one born, had always been the wildest, and John, the baby brother, had always been the gentlest, the kindest, the best. Maybe it was true that the good die young.

Maybe it was true that even if both of them were still here, neither would want to make the ranch his main concern for all his life. He, Clint, would just have to accept life the way it was.

Maybe if he made his challenges big enough, and took big enough risks to try to meet them, he'd forget all about this lonely funk he was in, and the ridiculous riding school, too.

The whole time he was visiting with Larry, though, he couldn't keep from glancing around for Cait from time to time. Just out of curiosity as to how she was handling herself. She did finally escape from the younger men but, just as she tried to slip out into the kitchen, his grandfather's old friend Mac Torrance caught up with her. Clearly he was asking her to dance but she refused him, too.

Finally he and Larry sealed the deal to book his three best mares and Clint moved on to visit with some other guests. The next thing he knew, the band was playing a fast song, LydaAnn and her friend Janie were starting a line dance and Cait had disappeared.

The noise level in the room rose another notch. At least it *sounded* like a merry Christmas Eve on the Rocking M, in spite of all the sadness of the year just past.

Bobbie Ann came by with a fresh platter of tortilla chips and her famous salsa dip.

"You'd better go get in that line and dance," she said. "Or your sisters will be on your case."

"I danced with Faylene. That's enough dancing for tonight."

"Delia and LydaAnn are trying so hard to make this be Christmas, Clint," she said, frowning. "Help 'em out all you can."

Irritation stabbed through him.

"I've been working this crowd like a politician," he snapped. "What more do they want?"

"How about a smile?" she said. "I'd like to see one of those from you, myself."

Thoroughly annoyed, he glanced away.

And there was Cait, standing alone in the book-lined alcove that held the Remington sculpture, thumbing through a book she'd opened on the table.

"Now, there's a family member—according to you, Ma," he said. "Why don't you go tell her to do her duty and get out there in line?"

Bobbie Ann gazed at him thoughtfully.

"She even refused to dance with poor old Mac," Clint groused. "It embarrassed him. And she hasn't talked to anyone but those kids with the Carmacks."

"I'm thinking this is all a bit overwhelming for Cait," his mother said softly. "Don't you think so? What with her background and all?"

Shame hit him again, like a fist to the gut. When it came to Cait, he was just piling up the guilt.

But he couldn't take his eyes off her. Standing there so still, looking down at that book so intently, she held her head at a vulnerable angle. The soft light limned her beautiful neck and shoulders, shadow fell across her face. She studied that book without moving a muscle.

"She isn't accustomed to big social gatherings," Bobbie Ann said softly. "Our Cait is a bit of a loner."

Our Cait. Clint didn't even challenge that. He was too busy trying to fend off the unnameable feelings washing through him as he looked at this Cait he'd never seen before.

Finally she felt his gaze. She glanced up and looked straight at him for a fleeting moment, acknowledging his existence with the most noncommittal of looks and for the barest fraction of a heartbeat in time.

Much as she had done when she first came into the room.

This time it stabbed him even deeper.

Then she looked at Bobbie Ann and smiled before she went back to slowly turning the pages.

"Let her be," Bobbie Ann murmured. "She likes to see the pictures of the family."

Only then did he notice that the large-paged book was not a picture book of Western art. It was one of the big leather photo albums embossed with the Rocking M brand that held the history of the McMahans.

Cait sat on the floor in the shadow of the huge Christmas tree and reached out to touch the papier-mâché cowboy ornament. He was twirling his red rope above his head in a perfect, huge loop. He was so old that the gold thread he was supposed to hang by from the center of his hat had worn in two and he stood bowlegged on a thick branch instead.

"I'll be very careful not to knock you off balance," she whispered.

No one was around to hear her, though. Almost all the guests had gone and Delia and her band had finished playing.

It was almost time for the family dinner.

But was she really one of the family? John was gone.

"John was one of the good guys, too," she told the cowboy. "He was the very best."

She drew up her knees and wrapped her arms around them while she stared at the tree. Maybe she'd just stay here and not go to dinner. At this moment she had no desire to eat.

The John McMahan Memorial School of Horsemanship.

That would look good over the gate to the arena. Or over the door of the barn.

She had loved John with all her heart. From the very first minute they'd met, two strangers sharing a table to eat pizza from a cart in the trade show at the Quarter Horse Congress, he had treated her as if she were a princess. John had been nicer to her than any other man she'd ever dated.

He'd been nicer to her than any other man she'd ever *known*.

His blue eyes had twinkled when he talked to her and his brown hair had lifted and fallen in the wind. Gently. John was a gentle man and a gentleman and she had loved him with her heart and soul.

She had never loved a man until she loved John.

But it was his big brother Clint who stirred her blood now.

Cait closed her eyes and pushed the feelings away—the feelings that tried to take her breath every time she even thought of Clint. She didn't know how to name them and she didn't even want to try.

All she knew for sure was that John had wanted her here, with his family. *In* his family.

Clint did not.

But she wouldn't think about Clint.

She drew in a deep breath of the wonderful, spicy smell of the tree. She looked up. It must be nine feet tall.

A storybook tree. For a storybook Christmas.

"Mer-ry Christ-mas! And to your mama and daddy, too!"

It was Bobbie Ann's voice, floating in from outside where she was saying goodbye to the last of the guests.

"Tell them we're so sorry they didn't feel up to coming with you all. I'll be over to see them soon."

John had told her that all the guests on Christmas Eve who came to the Rocking M with *their* guests were from families who'd been friends with the McMahans since the Comanches had signed a treaty with the first German settlers. The only treaty between Native Americans and Americans that had never been broken.

"Well," John had said, laughing, "actually it was between Native Americans and *Texans*. Maybe that's why."

She couldn't even imagine families who had known each other for so many years, for *generations*. Families who had grown and multiplied and become intertwined with all the others. Families who had lived in one county for a hundred and fifty years.

When her grandparents couldn't even stay in the same *country*. When her parents couldn't even keep the three of them together or stay in the same apartment for half a year.

John was gone.

Clint was here.

And she was here, in his home, with the first horses she had ever owned and the first important job that God had ever given her. The most important dream she'd ever set out to fulfill.

Clint wanted her gone.

Lord? You brought me here, didn't You? Isn't this where You meant for me to be? Maybe I was wrong about Clint. But isn't this where You sent me to make a mark for You?

Chapter Three

Clint showed the Tollivers to the door when they got ready to leave, and stood on the porch talking to them for a minute. Then, as soon as they said their last goodbyes, he headed for the barn.

"Hey," James Tolliver yelled as he wheeled his Escalade around the circle drive, "need some help with the chores?"

"No, thanks."

Clint waved him off and kept going. If he didn't get a few minutes alone, he was going to smother. And if he was checking the horses, his mother couldn't fuss at him about neglecting his duties as host. After all, she was the one who had insisted on giving every hand on the Rocking M the evening off for Christmas Eve.

He had to get away from her. And from his sisters, who were trying to *make* it be Christmas. They had worried about holiday celebrations for two years now, ever since Dad had died of a sudden heart attack.

He had to get away from them.

He had to get away from everybody.

He had to get away from Cait.

The truth of it shocked him. He surely wasn't leaving the house to avoid *Cait*.

But he was, and that brought an ironic grin to his lips. Cait wasn't exactly chasing him around the Christmas tree.

And he couldn't say that he blamed her.

Once inside the refuge of the big barn, he walked slowly down the aisle, looking into the stalls on each side, checking to see that no one was looking colicky and no one was out of water. Halfway down the show-horse side, he heard footsteps behind him.

Uneven footsteps. Finally. Jackson was here. Clint stopped and turned around.

"Well, it's about time you showed up!"

He ought to be angry with his tardy brother, but these days it was hard to be anything but glad whenever he saw him. Since he'd met Darcy and married her, it was as if the real Jackson had come back to life.

"Did you miss me, big brother?"

It was still a shock to get a response from Jackson, much less a cheerful one, after being accustomed to him staying locked in his own gloomy, reclusive little world for months and months after his terrible wreck.

"I could use a little help keeping the festivities

going," Clint said in the same light tone. "Right now I'm in trouble for refusing to line dance."

"Then let me at 'em," Jackson said. "I'll dance 'em right into the ground."

His limping gait brought him nearer, and Clint saw that he not only had a wide grin on his face, he had a twinkle in his eyes.

"I'm gonna go get the thermometer," he said. "I think you've got a fever."

"I do," Jackson said. "A fever named Darcy."

Clint threw back his head and laughed and laughed, which made him feel much better all of a sudden.

"You're over the edge, man, you're downright besotted. I never thought I'd see you in such a pitiful shape."

Jackson turned his hands—his *bare* hands—palms up.

"What can I say? I'm all hers. I live to please her."

"Hey, hey, get a grip," Clint said, grabbing his arm in mock panic. "Be sure not to tell *her* that!"

Jackson just grinned at him and Clint grinned back. Then he got serious and searched his face.

"No foolin', Jackson," he said. "You think she loves you as much as you love her?"

Still smiling, Jackson nodded.

"I know she does."

"*How* do you know?"

"I can tell. By the way she acts. By what she says."

When Clint just stared at him without saying any more, Jackson nailed him with a sharp look.

"How come you wanna know? You fallin' for somebody?"

He thought for a minute, then snapped his fingers as best he could.

"*Lorrie Nolan!* I heard you took her to Hugo's for breakfast the other day!"

Clint snorted.

"Are you and Lorrie…"

"No!"

"She'd be a good match for you—she's got a mind of her own."

"Yeah. A mind to be a McMahan."

Clint turned and started past the last half of the stalls.

"Check 'em on that side for me, will ya?" he said.

"Yeah. And you tell me what you're talkin' about, then, if it's not you and Lorrie."

Clint shrugged.

"Women in general, I guess," he said. "When they act like a different person than they ever did before, how d'you know which one's real?"

Then he snapped his jaw shut. He wasn't saying any more, no matter what, because this whole conversation was nothing but a stupid waste of breath. Jackson couldn't be a bit of help, anyhow, blindly in love with Darcy as he was.

But Jackson was silent, thinking about it.

"Well," he drawled at last, "I'd say, Clint, ol'

bro, if she's actin' like she never did before, she might have changed her mind. She may be trying to tell you somethin'."

By the time he and Jackson got to the house, only the immediate family, which included various relatives of Bobbie Ann's, was left. At least the evening was passing.

Everybody was standing around talking in the dining room or going in and out of it, bringing in food and lighting candles, and Aunt Faylene was at the sideboard taking the cover off one of her famous cakes. She turned and smiled at them as they walked in.

"My favorite nephews," she proclaimed. "I want a hug."

They gave her hugs and listened to her chatter for a minute, then she said, very low, "Any word from Monte?"

"Not that I know of," Clint said.

"You'd know," she said, her lips tightening. "Poor Bobbie Ann'd be walking on air if he'd called."

Her gaze went to her sister, just coming in from the kitchen with a huge crock of chili. Clint went to help her with it.

"Places, everyone," she called. "Time for dinner."

Clint set the crock in the middle of the long table and glanced around.

"Where's Cait?" he said.

No one knew.

"I'll get her," he said, and left the room.

First she wouldn't dance, then she wouldn't mingle and now she wouldn't come to dinner. What was she doing, anyhow? Bobbie Ann didn't need another worry, nor another absentee right now. He would say something to Cait. If she was going to accept an invitation, then she had an obligation...

The sight of her stopped him in his tracks.

She sat beside the Christmas tree with her knees drawn up and her arms wrapped around them, staring at it as if she were a little girl. Lost in its magic.

As he watched, she lifted one hand and fingered the glass bead on the simple necklace at her throat. She was gone someplace else, that was for sure. Dinner at the Rocking M was the furthest thing from her mind right now.

A thought came, unbidden. Was she thinking about John? Remembering times with him? Had they shared a mighty love like Darcy and Jackson's seemed to be?

His gut told him no. Darcy and Jackson were a matched pair. Anybody could spend five minutes with them and know that. John and Cait had been a whole different story.

She laid her head against her knees for a long moment, then lifted it and looked up at the angel at the top of the tree. The white profile of her face and throat was so pure and beautiful it made him swallow hard.

Slowly he walked across the room. She didn't

even hear his boot heels on the tiled floor. He reached the circle of light made by the tree and looked down at her sitting in its shadow.

"Cait?"

She started as if he'd waked her from sleep. A quick flash of fear crossed her face, then surprise. Was that a sheen of tears in her eyes?

It moved him. Against his will.

It made him want to protect her, somehow. Which was a laughable thought, for sure.

What was she afraid of? The Caitlin he knew wasn't scared of anything.

"Dinner's ready."

Cait wanted to get up. She really did. But Clint was so close she could smell his aftershave.

His gray eyes were so intense they seared her skin.

The heat rose up in her neck and her entire body tilted to feverish.

Just like early this morning when she'd walked in on him riding that colt.

Just like the moment, dear Lord help her, that she'd looked at him across the back of the black horse and told him, "Christmas Eve gift."

"Time for dinner," he said, as if she spoke a foreign language and he should try another phrase to convey the same information.

But she was frozen there, despite the blood pulsing through her veins hot enough to melt her.

He took a step closer, as if to see what was wrong, and for one instant she thought he was going to hold out his hand to help her up. For that same instant, she was ready to reach for it.

But he kept his hands at his sides.

"We'd better get in there," he said, in a tone so neutral she couldn't find his feelings in it, "or else Jackson will eat up all the tamales."

Her pulse was pounding so hard she was afraid he'd hear it and she stood still for a moment the instant she was on her feet. Trying to slow the blood in her veins. Trying to deepen the breaths in her body.

Even in that split second, though, while they stood near enough to touch, a deeper thrill went surging through her, the thrill of his closeness, the warm scent of him and the look in his eyes that tightened the unspoken tension that invariably vibrated between them. She cleared her throat and tried to speak normally.

"So," she managed to say in her coolest tone, "is that another family tradition I don't know? Last one to the table gets no tamales?"

He did have the grace to let her see his chagrin.

But he didn't apologize. Actually, she couldn't imagine Clint apologizing to her. Not for speaking his mind about his strong, true feelings that she didn't belong here.

She had to remember that. He thought she didn't belong here. He didn't want her here, no matter how gallantly he'd called her to dinner. He was the host, she was the guest.

Of his mother.

She walked past and left him to follow as she headed toward the rest of the family gathering around the table in the dining room. Delia's voice came to her clearly as she and Clint approached the door.

"...that time John was trying to steal my sopaipilla and I tried to spear it with my fork and stabbed him in the hand instead? That's what started the water fight of all time!"

"Ooh, yeah!" LydaAnn chimed in. "That was in Tulsa at the Fourth of July show. We had everybody at the stalls soaking wet before it was all over."

Jackson added something, too, but Cait barely heard it. She felt *she* was the one stabbed. That was a story John had never told her, had never even mentioned, and everyone else here knew all about it. Everybody in the family, judging from the number of voices recalling more details.

"I remember," Faylene said, "when Johnny was little and he'd string honey all over his sopaipilla and his plate and the table and everything else and refuse to pass it on and—"

She stopped talking the minute Cait stepped into the room. So did everybody else. No more talk about John. Or anything.

Just for one heartbeat.

"Ah, Cait, there you are," Bobbie Ann said, and indicated her place.

Clint held the chair for her before he went around to what must be his regular seat at the end of the long oak table.

"Let's hold hands and say the blessing."

They did. Cait had never heard that blessing. She didn't know the words.

Then Bobbie Ann began filling the brightly colored bowls with chili, one by one they passed them around the table, and everyone started talking at once. Faylene served the tamales from the pottery platter; they all passed around the huge salad and the salsas and quesos, chips, corn bread, tortillas, red, yellow and blue corn and flour ones, too, pico de gallo and guacamole.

Cait concentrated on the beautiful sight of the table and its bountiful, colorful food. She tried to fix her mind on what Faylene was telling her.

But from the way they talked and joked, she could tell that LydaAnn and Delia obviously were already closer friends with Jackson's new wife, Darcy, than they had ever been with her. And when she unexpectedly caught LydaAnn staring a hole through her with tear-filled eyes, the question she'd asked herself a thousand times popped into her mind again.

How many of the family members gathered around this table joined Clint in blaming her? How many of them thought John would still be alive if Cait had gone with him to Mexico?

After dinner they all cleaned up, really fast, because they had a system. All Bobbie Ann could think of for Cait to do was put a new batch of Christmas CDs in the player and light all the candles in the great room area near the tree. Smokey, Bobbie Ann's ancient cat, was the only one who helped her.

When she was finished, she picked up the cat and sat down in the chair nearest the tree. She could look at the twinkling lights, listen to the music and try not to think.

Let me have this moment, Lord, that You have given me. Don't let me look ahead. Don't let me look back to John.

Sometimes it was hard to remember exactly John's face. And his scent and his smile. Wasn't this what she'd always wanted—this family in this safe house, this kind of Christmas and this kind of life? Yes, but she wanted John here with her, too.

"The Lord helps those who help themselves," she whispered to the fat gray-and-white cat. "I'm not going to think about anything at all tonight so I can enjoy this time."

She stroked Smokey and listened to her purr.

"Clint's been going out to breakfast with Lorrie Nolan, I hear," Jackson announced loudly. "Did you know that, LydaAnn?"

Cait looked up to see them all coming in from the kitchen, Darcy and Jackson in the lead.

"Jackson, mind your own business," Clint called.

"Just trying to keep everybody up to date," Jackson said with a hearty chuckle. "How come you didn't ask her here tonight?"

"Because it'd make all his other women jealous," LydaAnn said cheerfully. "Isn't that right, Clint?"

"They're not my women," he said grumpily.

"They think they are," Delia said.

"They *think* they'd like to live on a ranch," Clint

said sharply, "and have good horses to show and plenty of money to spend and no job to go to. It's not me they're interested in."

"Clint, you are such a cynic!" LydaAnn said.

Clint shrugged. "That's right, isn't it, Jackson? The McMahan men are always magnets for that kind of women—we have been ever since high school."

He looked at Cait when he said it. It was a fleeting glance, but for a second he looked right at her. Her temper flared, and she opened her mouth, then snapped it shut again. This Christmas was already hard enough for Bobbie Ann. She would not be the one to make it harder.

"Well, thanks a lot, Clint!" Darcy said, pretending to be mightily offended as she settled in close beside Jackson on the leather love seat. "I, for one, am not that kind of woman. Why, I was trying to catch Jackson's eye when I thought he couldn't afford more than a wood stove to cook on and paper plates to eat on!"

"No, you weren't, you were after Bobbie Ann's cooking," Jackson said, putting his arm around her shoulders and pulling her even closer to him, "and my good horses. You fell in love with Stranger, that's how come you're still here."

Darcy looked up at him with such a smile and such a look in her eyes that it squeezed Cait's heart. John was gone forever.

"That's exactly what I said," Clint drawled. "They're all in it for the good horses. Forget us men."

"We-ell," Jackson said, "I don't know. From what Hugo told me, you and Lorrie—"

"Jackson," Clint interrupted firmly, "I'm thinking I liked you better when you were all sulled up and wouldn't say a word."

That brought the most genuine laughter of the whole evening, and more teasing for Clint from his sisters.

"Don't you discourage Jackson!" Bobbie Ann cried, but she was laughing, too. "You might make him revert to the bad old days!"

The phone rang then, and she jumped. She grabbed the cordless from the table beside her chair and the instant she put it to her ear, her face lit up.

"Monte!" she said.

Everybody went completely still, as if one movement from anyone would sever the connection. Bobbie Ann clasped the phone with both hands.

"We're missing you so much," she said, and then she bit her lip and hushed.

She listened, she made short comments, she smiled, but tears stood in her eyes.

"They're all here," she said, after only a moment or two. "Do you want to tell them yourself? I'll pass the phone around…. Oh, all right, darling. Well, then, know that we love you with all our hearts and merry Christmas to you, too, sweetheart."

She punched a button and let the phone fall into her lap. Then she just stared into space for a moment.

"Monte wishes all of us a merry Christmas," she said tightly. "He's on his way to Omaha."

Nobody said a word. Clint clenched his jaw, Jackson glowered, LydaAnn and Delia had tears in their eyes, but they both looked angry instead of sad. All four of Bobbie Ann's children looked absolutely furious, come to think of it.

"There's a big contest there tomorrow with lots of the gate money going to charity."

Still no response from anyone. Cait was mystified. John had told her he had another brother, Monte. And that Monte was gone a lot, riding on the Professional Bull Riders circuit. That was all she knew.

But everybody else here knew more. This wasn't just a sibling gone a lot. It was more than that.

She searched her memory. At the time of John's death, Monte had been the last thing on her mind, but they'd all been upset that he hadn't come home for the funeral. He'd been in Brazil, or somewhere in South America, she remembered vaguely, when they'd finally tracked him down. It was...he'd gone there with a Brazilian buddy from the PBR, or something like that.

The tense silence went on and on. Finally Jackson cleared his throat.

"Ma," he said, "Darcy and I have a gift for you."

Bobbie Ann took a deep breath, sat up straight and turned her blazing blue eyes onto her second son. She widened the smile.

"How nice," she said. "I can't wait to see it."

Jackson's face lost all its tension. He grinned at Darcy, who grinned back at him.

"Neither can we," he drawled.

"You mean you've brought me a pig in a poke?"

She spoke lightly but there was an undercurrent of quick, new excitement in her voice.

His grin broadened.

"You might say that."

He looked into Darcy's eyes again and then laid one of his big, scarred hands on her flat belly.

"We're going to have a baby," he said. "In August."

It took a couple of seconds for the electrifying news to soak in.

"Ooh!" LydaAnn squealed. "I can't wait, I can't wait!"

"A baby!" Bobbie Ann cried. "My first grand-baby!"

Suddenly all the McMahans—except Cait—were on their feet, hugging, crying, Clint slapping Jackson on the back and hugging Darcy, then the aunts and uncles joining in. Congratulations and questions flew in all directions.

"Reckon it's a girl or a boy?"

"What time in August?"

"How long have y'all known this and kept us in the dark?"

Cait sat and watched. She couldn't very well get up with the cat asleep in her lap.

Clint got a glimpse of Cait's face as he went to get the bag his mother had asked for from under the tree. That lost-little-girl look hadn't quite left her.

There she was again, refusing to join in with everybody else. It irritated him. It was the least she could do if she was going to accept Bobbie Ann's invitation.

But his conscience stabbed him again.

Cait had looked worried and mystified when Bobbie Ann was so upset after Monte's call. Her heart had gone out to his mother along with everybody else's.

He searched the piles of packages under and around the tree. For a second he couldn't quite think what she'd sent him for. Oh, yeah: big shiny red bag from Spirit of Texas Silver.

And there it was.

He picked it up and took it to Bobbie Ann without looking at Cait again.

"The Christmas Eve gifts are different for the girls and the boys this year," Bobbie Ann said as she started taking small, beautifully wrapped packages from the bag. "Boys' wrapped in silver, girls' in red. Except for that, it doesn't matter who gets which one."

Clint took a silver and a red box from Uncle Lawrence and turned to pass them on to Jackson and Darcy. He couldn't help but see Cait.

Darcy had just passed on a box to her. Cait glanced around, saw that this gift was hers to keep and, working with the fat old cat lying asleep in her lap, began to slip the ribbon off, because it was what was holding the box closed. Instead of untying the fancy bow, she was going to save it.

"Clint."

He turned to find Uncle Lawrence holding out a silver box to him.

"That one's yours, son," the old man said.

Clint took the box and looked at Cait again.

Smokey had woken up and was swiping at the bow, wanting to play. Cait smiled and slipped it onto her wrist for safekeeping, gave the cat a pat before she lifted the lid to the box.

Her face lit up and she took the gift out—must be a tree ornament, he thought, since it dangled from a loop of red-and-green-and-silver-braided ribbon. Silver horses running.

Cait looked at it, moving it so that it would catch the light, reaching to trace the edge of it with her free hand. She was wasting that famous smile of hers on an inanimate object.

Then she flashed a grateful look at Bobbie Ann that pierced his heart.

He was glad that Bobbie Ann saw it and smiled back.

Cait mouthed the words "Thank you."

Bobbie Ann nodded, and mouthed, "You're welcome," then she looked around, full circle, at her girls, at Clint and Jackson and Darcy, and back to Cait.

"I hope y'all enjoy them," she said, loud enough to be heard over all the voices. "Merry Christmas Eve from your mother."

Cait looked up at her quickly, almost as if to see if Bobbie Ann was talking to her, too.

He didn't even know if Cait had ever had a mother. Seemed as if she was raised by an aunt, or something. Bobbie Ann would know. It just made him mad that she'd had such a horrible childhood.

Angry at himself for even caring, he tore his gaze away from her and set it firmly on his own gift. Cait's childhood was none of his concern. And neither was her present.

He ripped away the ribbon—with no fancy bow for the men—and took the lid off.

It was an ornate silver money clip embossed with the Rocking M brand cut out of gold and edged with black. His Christmas Eve gift.

"I hope you're not including me in that mothering thing," Faylene was saying dryly. "You boss me around enough as big sister, never mind mother."

That made Bobbie Ann laugh, which, Clint realized when he glanced at his aunt, was the purpose.

"Good try, Faylie," Bobbie Ann said, "but everybody here already knows you're older than I am. A lot older."

Cait was still staring at her gift. It was lying on her knee, shining bright against the soft black velvet of her skirt. She was running her fingers over the fine, delicately wrought horses with their manes and tails flying like flags. She was lost in another world, completely oblivious to the talking and laughing and milling around of the others in the room.

Totally unaware of his eyes on her.

Probably she had never received very many gifts in her life.

Probably *he* had never been as rude to any other woman in *his* life.

He got up and walked across the room.

"Are these ornaments a hint, Bobbie Ann?" Faylene was saying. "Are you saying that you hope someday we'll put up our own trees and invite everyone to *our* houses so you don't have to make chili?"

"I'd make chili anyhow," Bobbie Ann said. "My fans would demand it."

Clint reached Cait's chair and stopped in front of it.

She looked up. The expression in her eyes wasn't dreamy at all. It was thoughtful. And determined.

"Clint."

She said his name in a tone that cooled all the warm feelings he was having for her.

Then she continued to look up at him with her perfectly arched black eyebrows slightly raised. As if he should explain himself.

Faylene and Bobbie Ann had stopped talking. They, too, were no doubt looking at him and wondering what he was doing.

"Here," he said, offering Cait the money clip. "You claimed my Christmas Eve gift this morning, so it's yours."

She looked at him with her incomparable straight, haughty look.

"Keep it," she said. "I have my own."

"Well, I have the ranch," he snapped. "So you keep this."

He dropped it into her lap, turned on his heel and walked out, narrowly missing the startled cat, who'd jumped to the floor.

Chapter Four

At least they wouldn't have to sit down together for Christmas breakfast. Clint thought about that as he took the eggs from the refrigerator and dug around in the cabinet for the bowl he liked to beat them in.

He wouldn't have to say a word to Cait—in fact, it'd be easy to ignore her completely, as he'd done so far this morning. Late this afternoon, at dinner, he'd be acting as host and they'd all be around the table and that might require a polite remark or two, but basically, he was through being nice to her. That abrupt rejection of his Christmas Eve gift had been the last straw.

She was the rudest woman he'd ever met, bar none.

He found the bowl and his omelette pan and set to work.

For Christmas-morning breakfast, the tradition

was that Clint made omelettes, Jackson made and served coffee, and the main treat was the braided raisin bread Bobbie Ann made during the holiday season, slices warmed in the oven with butter. Darcy was in charge of that this morning. Normally it was John's job with Monte watching the oven, because the purpose was to give all the women a break from cooking.

So they could save their energy to cook the Christmas dinner, his dad had always said. He had said the same thing every year, with one of his big, booming laughs, as he'd bustled around stacking plates on the center island and getting out the silverware and helping his boys. They'd started that when Clint was nine years old and needed to stand on a stool to reach the stovetop.

He finished beating the first batch of eggs and poured them into the pan. He was thankful to have Jackson back, but he missed Dad and John and Monte with a sharp ache in his gut. If he ever saw Monte again, he wouldn't be responsible for what he might do. He was liable to knock him right into next week.

Clint jerked his mind back to the present.

It was nearly over. The gift exchange was finished, breakfast soon would be, and then he could do as he pleased until dinner. Maybe after that Cait would go back to her room or apartment or wherever she lived at Roy's.

Fat chance. With her seven new horses right here

on the Rocking M, she'd naturally want to try them all out.

He set his jaw. Instead of past years and people being gone, the main thing he'd better be thinking about was who was here—and how to get *her* to go away.

What he was going to do was get her and those horses *off* the Rocking M, and do it just as soon as humanly possible. As soon as Christmas was over—tomorrow morning—he'd talk to Bobbie Ann and tell her his idea. He'd play up the conflicts Cait would cause with the trainers and the extra work for Manuel's crew, plus the problems a bunch of kids could cause.

Screams and a loud burst of giggles erupted at the center island of the big kitchen.

"Watch it, Delia! You never could do the oranges. If you squirt me in the eye one more time, you're outta here."

"Not on Christmas," Delia drawled, completely unperturbed. "You can't throw me out on Christmas morning. That'd be too pitiful."

LydaAnn squealed.

"Again! You did it again. That was on purpose, and you can't tell me it wasn't...."

Darcy's husky voice interrupted the sisterly squabble.

"Now, now. I'll make peace," she said from her post by the oven. "How about trading with Delia, Cait? She can do the grapes."

"Santa put apples in the stockings," Delia said,

"because he knows I've been a good girl and I don't like to do the grapes. Hand me an apple, will you, Cait?"

"Here you go," Cait said. "Santa left a note that said chop it up with the peel on if you want."

Her voice was easy and relaxed.

Clint tilted the pan, slid the spatula under the eggs and turned them.

"And give me the oranges," Cait's beautiful voice said. "Quick, before LydaAnn gets them. She might give you an orange juice bath for revenge."

Delia said, "Cait! Shh! Don't give her any ideas!"

Clint's blood grew a little colder with every word they spoke—they were carrying on as if they were all the best of friends. This could be a problem. It'd be hard enough to convince Bobbie Ann to agree that he should push Cait and her school off the ranch, much less have to contend with his sisters, to boot.

If he could just get through this day, then everything would be back to normal. He hoped. Holidays should be banned so there would be nothing but normal workdays, one after another, with no traditions or celebrations or visiting ex-sisters-in-law.

Christmas breakfast was always eaten individually, when the next omelette came out of the skillet—at the table by the wide windows or perched at the breakfast bar or sitting on the antique bench by the back door. Everyone munched on fruit and the braided bread, toasted or not, while waiting around for eggs. When they were children, they'd loved the freedom of eating wherever they chose or not eating at all while they'd played with their new toys.

Evidently that was another tradition LydaAnn was holding on to.

"Cait, I just love my new hair clasp," she said. "Look how great these colors are in my hair."

Clint glanced over his shoulder. LydaAnn was twisting her neck, trying to see herself in the horn-framed mirror that hung over the bench.

"I thought they'd be perfect for you," Cait said. "I really had fun picking out all the gifts."

"Hitching horsehair takes a long time," LydaAnn said. "I don't see how Billy Ross can hitch fast enough to keep a shop open."

"He can't. He's getting free rent from that sad-dlemaker," Cait said. "The seven things I bought put quite a dent in his stock."

"Well, they're all beautiful," Darcy said. "He's very good at it."

"I'm hoping to have him come out and give a demonstration for my students," Cait said. "Who knows? Some of them might want to take up hitching."

Clint shook his head. That showed Cait was living in a dream world. Hitching horsehair took a lot of skill and a lot of patience. Why would rich kids who could buy anything they wanted even think about trying to learn it?

"When are you starting your classes?"

That was Darcy, keeping up with the conversation

even though she was halfway across the room. When had Cait told her about her school?

He didn't need Darcy and Cait getting all friendly, either, because he'd been encouraging Jackson to help run the ranch again, at long last. It'd be a real fiasco if Darcy pushed Jackson to support Cait's school as his first contribution to management.

"As soon as the horses have a few days to get used to being in a new place," Cait said. "And I need to ride them all some more and get to know them better."

"Want some help?" said LydaAnn.

"Sure," Cait said. "If you want. That'd be great."

Her voice held surprise and pleasure. And pure determination to go right on ahead with all her plans.

She knew he was standing here listening. She knew she was twisting the knife.

Oh, yes. The old Cait in starched jeans and shirt was back with them today—the vulnerable one who wore silk and velvet was gone.

Well, this particular challenge was too much. Christmas or not, he'd better nip all this sisterhood in the bud or she'd have her roots down deep and everyone else on the ranch on her side.

Bobbie Ann came in from the great room at that exact moment. He might as well get his show on the road.

"You know, Cait," he said, glancing at her as he slid the omelette onto a warm plate and handed it to his mother, "I've been thinking that you really need an indoor arena for your school. I'll be glad to make arrangements for you to use the one at the fairgrounds.''

When she didn't answer, he turned around to see her staring at him with her straight, determined look.

"That way, you won't have to worry about liability or anything like that, and your students will have plenty of parking.''

Now his sisters and Darcy were looking at him, too.

"Very thoughtful of you, Clint,'' Delia said sarcastically. "All she'd have to do would be load up her horses and seven saddles and haul them thirty miles to the fairgrounds every day.''

"My reaction exactly,'' Cait said, turning her great dark eyes onto Delia.

Delia met her gaze with a significant look of her own.

Clint's temper flared.

Was this some kind of a female conspiracy?

"Well,'' he said irritably, "your little girls'd be a whole lot more comfortable if they were out of the sun and wind. I'd think it'd be worth it.''

He started to turn back to reach for the egg carton and saw Bobbie Ann's blue eyes fixed on him.

She looked at him thoughtfully for a long moment, then carried her plate to the bar and climbed up onto a bar stool beside Cait. The women went on with their chatter and their fruit chopping.

Jackson poured his mother some coffee and took it to her.

Clint watched him from the corner of his eye.

The least Jackson could do, after dumping all the decision-making for the ranch onto Clint for a year and a half—or more—was to put in a few words right now in defense of his brother's idea. *Why* hadn't he grabbed his opportunity in the barn last night and filled Jackson in on this whole crazy notion of Cait's? If Jackson knew everything, and thought it all through, he'd say it was a bad deal, too.

But everybody, Jackson included, seemed to have totally dismissed Clint's suggestion.

He beat the eggs an unnecessarily long time. Finally he poured them into the pan and turned to see Cait. She was completely immersed in her grape cutting.

"Have you ever run a riding school?" he said.

The question came out more abruptly than he'd intended and Bobbie Ann looked up from her plate, startled, and kept her eyes on him as she lifted her coffee cup to her lips. He pretended not to notice.

Cait glanced up at last, her black brows arched in surprise.

"Are you talking to me?" she said.

"Yes," he snapped.

"No," she said mildly. "Have you?"

He set his jaw to try to hold his temper. The woman was enough to make a man punch a hole right through the wall.

"No, but anybody knows that you can't keep students if you don't make them as comfortable as possible," he said.

"I've never run a school, but I've been a horse-crazy kid," Cait said thoughtfully. "Horses are the important thing. It'd take a blizzard or a tornado to make my students notice the weather."

Clint let her see his disbelief.

"Cait, it's obvious you don't have a clue what you're doing."

He turned back to his work.

Again they all started talking about something else.

"Trey Sanders has an indoor at the sale barn that he rents by the hour," Clint said, whirling on his heel to face them again. "That's a lot closer than the fairgrounds."

All of them looked at him now. He could feel Jackson and Darcy's eyes on him, although he didn't turn to see them.

"Clint," Bobbie Ann drawled, "in case you haven't noticed, the Rocking M also has an indoor."

She set down her coffee cup and smiled at him, but she had that look in her eye he'd known all his life. Trouble, it said. There'd be trouble if he didn't shape up.

His spine stiffened. He was the one running this ranch. He was the one responsible for its reputation, its profits, its people and its animals. For its very future—after five generations.

He was the one who would decide what took place inside its fences.

And he was the one who'd been so stupid as to push this disagreement about Cait's ridiculous school to a head on Christmas morning in front of the whole family. He couldn't back down now.

"The indoor at the Rocking M is in use 24/7," he said flatly, replying to Bobbie Ann but looking straight at Cait. "We have two professional trainers, two assistant trainers, their customers and the ranch employees in there already. There's no room or time for a riding school."

"I *told* you I'll use the old outdoor arena," Cait said. "I won't bother anyone. The Lord has laid it on my heart to establish this school and to do it on the Rocking M."

She held his furious gaze with a completely calm one of her own.

"It's a living memorial to John. The John McMahan Memorial School of Horsemanship."

Clint could do nothing but stare at her. He couldn't even breathe, because the words hit him like a fist to the solar plexus.

No, they were more like a stab in the back. One thing he'd never thought Cait to be was sneaky, but this proved she was that, too.

He'd known she was smart—her marrying into the McMahans when she and John were so mismatched proved that—but he hadn't known she was devious. Nothing else, absolutely *nothing* else, could make it truly impossible for him to persuade Bobbie Ann that this school would be bad for the Rocking M.

"Why didn't you tell me that?"

He glared at her. Fiercely. She stared right back. She didn't turn a hair.

"You didn't seem interested," she said in her cool way.

He looked around the room, at the faces of his family.

"Did y'all know this?" he snapped.

It was a horrible feeling that took precedence over all the confusion and anger and frustration swirling through him at that instant. A trapped feeling. Here he was, responsible for everything that happened on this ranch, yet he had no control over this situation and couldn't seem to get any.

Now there'd be no way to get rid of Cait. *Establish,* she had said. That sounded permanent. She'd be here forever and he was helpless to do the slightest thing about it.

Because his mother, his sisters, Darcy—even Jackson, for goodness sake—were all misty-eyed and sentimental, looking at her, thinking about John. He gritted his teeth. Couldn't they see that Cait had no right to be setting up a memorial to John when she hadn't even cared enough to go to Mexico with him?

"Did y'all *know* this?" he demanded again.

"I did," Bobbie Ann said, "and I think it's so unselfish and generous of Cait. After all, she works hard, long hours every day for Roy, and the school will take up all her leisure time."

Clint couldn't speak or he would explode. He

couldn't look at his mother another minute or he would say something completely inappropriate for Christmas morning.

Yet his heart was torn to shreds by the expression on her face and the tears in her eyes as she remembered John. If he had waited until tomorrow, it wouldn't have helped. The loss of her youngest son would always be fresh to her heart and there would never be a time that she'd be able to apply her natural business sense to anything connected with his memory.

He wouldn't be surprised if Bobbie Ann decided they should build another indoor arena just for Cait's school, invite her and all the students to supper every day and throw in a dozen new saddles and transportation to all the shows just to make them feel welcome. Cait certainly knew how to tug at Bobbie Ann's heartstrings.

Yep. It looked as if Cait was going to be a permanent fixture around here and there wasn't a blessed thing he could do about it. What *was* it about Cait? How could she have the power to turn him inside out like this?

When she reached the barn and saw her own horses standing there in a double row looking back at her, Cait stood still and took in a long, deep breath that settled her, at least a little bit. Those muscles felt unused, as if she hadn't breathed for a long time.

It was hard to breathe and walk the edge of a cliff at the same time.

"Why would I feel that way?" she said.

Nobody knew. All the big brown eyes looked at her sympathetically but nobody answered.

"I could take the school someplace else and it wouldn't kill me," Cait said. "Falling off a cliff probably would."

On closer observation, she saw that the buckskin mare had a different look in her eye. One that was more challenge than sympathy.

Cait walked toward her, thankful to think about horses instead of people.

"So you'd like to see what'd happen if I did take a fall?" she said.

She stood in front of the stall and let the mare sniff her hand and take in her scent.

"I may have to make you an intermediate horse, hmm? You could be too lively for the beginners. Is that what you're telling me?"

She scratched the mare's poll for a minute or two, then went to her trailer for the saddle and her longe line. The seller had told her the buckskin mare's barn name was Daisy. That could be because this mare was a deep yellow color—or it could be because she was fresh as a daisy every time anybody stepped up on her.

Cait let Daisy stand saddled and tied while she petted each of the others for a moment, then turned them out into their runs. She started with Daisy by clipping the longe line to her halter and leading her out to the old arena.

Standing in the middle of it, smooching to Daisy

to trot a big circle around her, Cait tried to let herself relax. Tried to fix her thoughts on this one horse and nothing else.

After a few circles, when she urged Daisy to canter, the mare resisted. Cait stepped forward and waved the end of the longe line, called to her, and she moved on out.

"Are you a little bit lazy, in spite of the spark in your eye?"

Daisy didn't answer, but she didn't have to. Fairly soon Cait called "Whoa."

Happily Daisy stopped. Time to ride.

Daisy did buck, halfheartedly, and she did try to run away, a little more earnestly, but basically she was lazy and when she couldn't bluff easily, she settled down and turned into a docile, willing mount.

Unfortunately that left Cait's worried mind free to begin torturing her again. She had known, and known for sure, that she was right to set up her school on the Rocking M before Clint had so scornfully tossed that money clip in her lap last night.

At that moment she realized that that knowledge only made things worse, for now she had no choice.

It had all become an even deeper dilemma when she'd told Clint the name of her school. He'd given her an absolutely murderous look. Clint did *not* want her here.

Lord, if You mean for me to be here, then why don't I feel welcome? Why do I feel so scared this won't work?

And why do I even care what Clint wants when I

*know now he won't try to throw me off the place?
I saw him give that up this morning when he looked
at his mother's face.*

God must get really tired of her asking why all
the time. Faith—that's what she needed. More faith.

*Let me give this worry to You, Lord. Let me give
it to You and let it go.*

She tried to focus on doing just that while she
rode. Finally, though, snippets and images from last
night and this morning kept creating more questions
in her heart. Was there anyone in this family who
really wanted her to be there?

Bobbie Ann did, but that really had nothing to do
with Cait herself. Cait was a way for her to hold on
to John.

Delia and LydaAnn and Darcy had been warm
and friendly while they made the fruit salad and after breakfast, too, when they had all worked together
to clean up the kitchen and the wrapping papers in
the great room. But they probably were just being
polite. They would have behaved the same way with
any houseguest.

And Clint. Clint had given up even the pretense
of politeness toward her.

Clearly he didn't even want a living memorial to
John if she came with it.

Why hadn't she told him the name of the school
yesterday, when she first told him she was starting
it?

Her mind skittered away from that question. That
didn't matter; no sense thinking about it.

What she had to remember was that God wanted her here. It didn't matter whether Clint did or not.

But Lord, I did hear You right? Here, on the Rocking M, on Christmas morning, I feel more alone than ever.

Restlessly she rode to the arena gate, leaned over to open it and sidepassed Daisy through it.

"Good girl. Very good. You know a lot of things."

It was true. The seller had not lied to her. These horses would be good with the kids.

She closed the gate and had the mare stand there for a long time, letting her get used to her surroundings outside the pen.

Letting *herself* look around at the immaculate ranch and drink in its beauty. The Rocking M could be featured in a magazine—it was that pretty, and yet it was completely functional, a blend of old and new. Limestone and rough cedar. Perfectly groomed white gravel and black asphalt roads and parking lots.

Flashes of bright reds and blues and whites in the flags flying high in front of the indoor arena: United States, Texas and Rocking M. She'd loved this place from the very first minute John had driven her onto it.

Slowly she eased the mare on out, went through another gate and trotted her into the big pasture of rolling hills that spread for many acres along the north side of the ranch headquarters. At the top of the first ridge she stopped, turned the mare and looked back at the house, then let her gaze wander across the Rocking M for as far as she could see.

The best old part of the ranch was the chapel over by Jackson's house. Now Jackson and Darcy's. Maybe she'd go there later today, after Christmas dinner. Or maybe she'd go now.

Christmas on the Rocking M hadn't turned out to be quite what she'd expected, especially when she remembered Clint throwing the money clip in her lap. Just thinking about it made her go cold and then hot with anger.

Yes, he did have the real ranch. No, he didn't need to carry the symbol of it in his pocket.

But he didn't have to be so hateful about it.

Lord, I'm going to kneel at the altar of the old chapel and ask You again, one more time. Is the Rocking M really where I belong?

Clint leaned against a post of the back porch and stared off across the rolling pasture. Cait was sitting her horse out there on the ridge like a Comanche sentinel and had been for the longest time. It was a standoff.

A remarkably ironic one, if he really thought about it. She was a Comanche—Aunt Faylie had already said so, hadn't she?—and he was the rancher on the edge of the frontier ready to defend his home.

Except that she had no prior claim on the land and he had no hope of negotiating a treaty that could help him in any way.

Finally, when he thought they'd be frozen like

this forever, she turned her horse and rode away. Just before she dropped over the rim of the hill she turned and looked back over her shoulder, once, as if she couldn't decide whether to go or stay.

He didn't know whether she'd seen him or not, as far away as she was. Or whether she'd recognized him if she'd seen him.

There'd been no doubt in his mind it was Cait.

He hadn't watched her leave the house, he hadn't asked anyone her whereabouts, he had simply known who it was as soon as he'd glimpsed the horse and rider heading away toward the hills. That had been from a long way away.

Far enough away that he hadn't actually *seen* that it was Cait. It was more that he had *known* it was Cait by some mysterious electrical impulse that traveled through the air.

He smiled bitterly to himself.

Everybody else in the family was happy to have this memorial to John, and he should be, too. But he couldn't even think about John. All he could think about was Cait and what she was about to do to his life. His ranch.

Honestly, he didn't care if there ever *was* a memorial to John if it meant she'd be here all the time. How selfish was that?

Again, the unthinkable thought hit him. He didn't know himself anymore. Normally he was unselfish, but then again, he was normally in control, too.

Behind him, the screened door creaked. Instinctively he whipped his head around to see who was there, as if he were afraid of being attacked.

He felt his mouth curve in a sheepish grin, it made him feel so ridiculous.

Bobbie Ann gave him a slight smile in return.

"Don't let me bother you," she murmured. "I just want to sit for a minute."

The soft words rang in his ears like a scream. His mother was a whirlwind, all the time. She always had been. She *never* wanted to just sit.

She walked past him, went halfway down the long porch and sat in one of the slatted cedar rocking chairs. Its high back and wide arms made her look even smaller than usual.

Had she come out here to talk to him, to try to make peace between him and Cait? To ask him to be nicer to her?

Guilt touched him with a cold hand. But then his natural stubbornness overcame it and he set his jaw. He didn't want to hear it.

And, evidently, she didn't want to say it, either. She rocked slowly, back and forth, back and forth and stared out across the hills.

He leaned against the post again and looked out at the spot he had been perusing in the peaceful blue sky. They stayed that way for a long time.

She was miffed at him, though, he could tell.

Well, if he wasn't going to throw Cait's school off the ranch, which he could not do without grieving his mother more, he should begin a conversation with her about it. That way he could set some parameters for the school's operations and Cait's involvement with the Rocking M.

Bobbie Ann continued to rock. Her thoughts seemed as long and far away as her blue gaze into the distance.

Finally he spoke.

"Cait rode off toward the chapel," he said. "She used to talk about restoring it. *That* would be a good memorial for John."

Bobbie Ann rocked forward one more time, set her feet on the floor and stood up. She walked to the edge of the porch, still staring out at the horizon.

"There are others who'd profit from a trip to the chapel," she said.

Chapter Five

When Cait rode up to the chapel, she stopped out in its yard and sat her horse, just looking at the weathered adobe building with the white cross on top. During the few months she'd been married to John and lived on the ranch, she had talked of restoring the chapel completely as a gift to him—it was his favorite place on the whole ranch—but then suddenly he was gone.

John. He had loved her for herself, her real self. He was the only man she'd ever known who took the trouble to know who she really was, deep inside.

He had loved her more than she had ever hoped to be loved.

So how could she, ungrateful wretch that she was, now feel such an attraction to Clint? She had to stop it. It made her feel that she was being unfaithful to John's memory—even to her quest to create the school as a tribute to him.

She had left the Rocking M right after John's funeral, desperately needing her old life back with its constant hard work. That was the only way she could keep from thinking and grieving too much. Now the school could serve that same function of keeping her feelings at bay.

Never, ever during her hard-won growing up had she let her feelings take over her life. She wasn't going to start now.

All she had to do was recognize this insane attraction to Clint and control it, and eventually it would go away. If she could control her grief—and the occasional flashes of guilt that said maybe John would still be alive if she'd gone with him—then she certainly could control her reactions to Clint. Not only to the attraction she felt toward him, but also to his antagonism.

The mare dropped her head, as if to graze, and Cait stepped off her to exchange the bit and bridle for the halter she'd brought along.

"You're probably wanting to lie down instead of eat, lazy rascal girl that you are," she said, patting Daisy's neck. "But I'm going to tie you to a tree so I can be sure you'll wait for me."

Even after she'd secured her mount, though, she walked only part of the way up the path to the wide oak doors fastened by an iron hook. All the weeds were cut down. The path and the entryway were swept. The cross on top shone a brighter white.

Darcy and Jackson had been married here, so they'd done all this for their wedding. However, it looked as if they were keeping it up. Her restoration plans for the chapel were being taken over by somebody else.

Which was fine. She'd been thankful to be out of town at a show when Darcy and Jackson got married, because of all the memories of John the chapel would have brought back to assault her again, but she had been compelled, somehow, to come here on this Christmas morning.

Would going inside make all her grief—and guilt—for John fresh again? That was her fear.

Dear God, help me if it does.

The minute she laid her hand on the ancient, worn wood of the door, warmed by the sunshine, she knew He was with her. He had brought her here.

She lifted the hook and let the doors swing wide.

The sunlight streamed in down the one center aisle and pooled at the plain and simple altar at the front. Nothing else was there. Only the rows of old oak benches and the altar.

Slowly Cait entered and walked down the aisle. She knelt at the altar.

She wanted to cry suddenly, she wanted to pray aloud, she wanted to run away from the hurt that Clint had dealt her last night. It all flooded back through her before she even thought of it again.

It was so heavy it weighed down her voice.

Lord, forgive my doubts, but please tell me one more time You mean for me to have my school on the Rocking M.

She closed her eyes and concentrated on opening her whole self to listen.

If You do, You'll have to help me bear the pain if Clint keeps on hating me so.

After a few moments she rose and sat on the front bench, staring into the pool of yellow sunshine, feeling the ancient walls around her. Hate and love were both so mysterious.

When John had asked her to marry him, so soon after they'd met, she hadn't known if she loved him enough. She'd told him so.

And he had convinced her that he had love enough for both of them. And he had. Until there'd come a point, on the way to take their vows, when she'd realized she *did* love him enough—she loved him mightily for his kind, gentle nature, for his wonderment at life and for the way he reflected her goodness in his eyes. John was the first person who had made her feel that she was a worthy human being.

And now Clint was making her feel that she wasn't.

But she *was*—God told her so. She wouldn't let her feelings about Clint rule her life, either. When she was near him, she had a dozen different feelings about him every minute.

Lord, should I have stayed away?

For a long time she sat there, then she got up and walked back up the aisle. Sometimes God answered right back, but rarely. That was one thing she had learned since her faith had begun growing from the tiny seed John had planted in her heart.

She reached for the small globe of glass at the hollow of her throat that held the real mustard seed he had given her.

Her heart stopped. It was gone!

She stood still, feeling her neck as if she could find the delicate gold chain somewhere against her skin. It was her most precious memento of John and she'd never been without it since he had given it to her.

Quickly she turned and retraced her steps to the altar, searching the aisle and the floor beneath the pews. Nothing. It was gone.

Standing helplessly at the front of the chapel, she felt a sudden peace. That little mustard seed was only a symbol. Her real faith was in her heart, its growth there started by John's own faith. Her real faith she could never lose.

Lord, let me remember that. Let me put my faith to good use and let me know if the Rocking M is the place I should do it.

She waited there for a long moment, then she turned and walked toward the open doors. Usually it took a while to hear from God and usually His direction came in an unexpected way.

In the wide doorway, underneath the big beam set into the adobe to form the top of the portal, she stopped and stood in the warm sunshine. This chapel had stood for more than a hundred years. Many seekers had come here, the very same way she had come—hurting and trusting at the same time. She could feel their spirits around her.

This place held a peace that she could almost touch.

So she walked to the steps and sat down to watch her mare doze in the sun, one hind foot cocked to rest.

Daisy looked a little bit scruffy, and even on her best day she couldn't compete with world-class horses like the ones produced and trained on the Rocking M. A lot of people might not like her personality. But nobody's opinion mattered if she brought the thrill of learning to ride to a kid who had no access to a horse.

Cait smiled at her.

"You're going to do some good for some kid," she murmured. "Maybe for a lot of kids, Daisy."

Clint would turn up his nose at the mare's appearance, but that didn't matter.

She had bought good, solid horses with the right dispositions for beginning riders. It had been so unusual to find that many of them in one lot and not have to search all over seven states for them. Because she hadn't wanted to pay the price for retired show horses, and it was hard to get mounts that were thoroughly broke like these.

It had been such a coincidence that one of Roy's customers from Tulsa, Mary Engles, had happened to call the very day Cait had felt compelled to go ahead with her school. And then Mary had mentioned these horses in a totally offhand way, without having a clue that Cait had a need for them.

It had been like a miracle.

That thought wafted through her head with the breeze that rustled the leaves of the mesquite bushes beside her.

It had *been* a miracle.

And with that realization, Cait knew God's hand was in it all and that she was where she was meant to be. Bobbie Ann welcomed her here, and everyone else but Clint seemed fine with it.

Clint's opinion—and her insane attraction to him—didn't matter. The school was the important thing, and not just as a memorial to John. Horses and faith could work more miracles in these children's lives than she could even imagine.

Her hurt didn't matter. God would bring her through it, just as He'd brought her through everything else.

The peace of the chapel filled her heart.

She could manage Clint. She had much more important things to do than worry about him.

Clint went back to his regular routine the next morning. In fact, he got up even earlier than usual to escape his awful dreams. In one of them—the one that finally woke him—Cait and Bobbie Ann kept insisting that he try to teach team-roping to a gaggle of little girls all dressed in English riding attire.

Then Delia and LydaAnn joined them to shamelessly make fun of his hopeless efforts.

Yep. Cait had stepped right into the middle of his life and made him look like a jackass, even to his mama. His subconscious was trying to tell him something, all right—she was about to create some situations on this ranch that he'd have to get her out of, a bunch of problems he'd have to solve.

But the biggest problem of all was his own personal one, and it was already in full bloom: the insane, all-consuming attraction he felt for her. The inexplicable need to be near her that had grabbed him in a vise grip the minute he saw her standing there leaning on the fence on Christmas Eve and had not let go of him since.

The answer to Delia's question.

"Look, Clint, what *is* your problem?" she had demanded after the Christmas-morning scene in the kitchen. "If you think this riding school of Cait's is such a stupid idea, why don't you just let it fail on its own?"

And he had not been able to reply. Not to the disgust in her voice or the concern in her eyes.

Honestly, the school was the least of his worries. He simply couldn't bear to be this close to Cait every day and not try to get even closer. *To his brother's wife.*

Blindly he reached for his clothes as he faced his troubling thoughts.

He might not be able to make her move her school off the ranch, but he most certainly could dictate the terms for it to stay.

And he would. Today. The minute she came

around poking her nose into *his* business, he'd tell her in no uncertain terms how to run *hers*. Maybe he could make her give up the whole idea and go away.

Clint buttoned his jeans and thrust his belt through the loops, jammed his feet into his work boots and tucked in his shirt as he left the room. He glanced down the hall toward Cait's room—it wouldn't surprise him a bit to see her coming out to torment him even this early in the day.

He couldn't get out of the house fast enough, since she was still in it. Ignoring the coffeepot on the counter, he crossed the kitchen in a few long strides and then the mudroom, where he grabbed his jacket from a peg by the door. Coffee in the barn would be fine. What he wanted was to get a couple of those colts ridden before he had an audience.

If she dared come to watch him ride today, he'd tell her to leave. He could do *that,* for sure—throw her out of the indoor while he was using it.

Crossing the frosty ground from the house to the main barn, he realized he didn't even know what time it was. But it was early, the sky barely beginning to show a pink light, so early not a single light shone inside any house on the ranch.

Of course, he couldn't see Jackson and Darcy's house. The lovebirds were most likely snuggled deep in their bed with sweet dreams of each other and the baby to come.

He felt a twinge of something strange—a feeling almost like jealousy. As the oldest son, he'd always expected the first grandchild to be his, to be the next Clint McMahan. Somewhere in the back of his mind without really thinking of it consciously, he had just assumed that was the way it would be.

Now the first child of the next generation would be Jackson's and probably none would be his. He couldn't imagine what it would be like to really be in love or have someone love him.

No, it wasn't a wife he wanted. What he wanted was to put the Rocking M at the top of all the best ranches in the country, and he wasn't going to let Cait and her shenanigans disrupt any of the programs he had set in motion.

Forget the programs and plans. The Rocking M, this eternal land, was what he loved.

He glanced out across the dimly peaceful expanse of grass that lay between the manager's house and the river, then turned his head to see if he could take in the high bluff rising along the north side of the valley. Its rocks and trees were just emerging from the grayness of first dawn. In spots, though, here and there, they shimmered pink and sparkling white as the frost reflected new light.

Tears sprang to his eyes. Much as he sometimes felt hopelessly tied to it, this place filled his heart.

In the barn he flipped on the light in the spacious headquarters office and then in the small kitchen. Automatically he ground the beans and started the coffee perking, then went out and down the aisle. He grinned. Midnight was awake and alert and ready to go.

The whole time he saddled and rode, though, it wasn't the same. He couldn't relax. Every time a shadow moved, he thought it might be Cait.

After all, she was the only one who knew about his private rodeo, and any minute she might appear. His secret wasn't a secret anymore and that ticked him off as much as the fact that she was here—and would be here every day, tempting him to touch her without even knowing that she was doing it.

Midnight bucked, Clint stayed on and they had a rousing ride, all to themselves. Much to his surprise.

"Feels almost lonesome in here, doesn't it, Midnight?"

The colt swung his head around and looked at him suspiciously.

"Just kidding, just kidding," Clint said as they continued loping around the arena. "Let's enjoy our privacy while we have it."

After that, Clint drank coffee in the office and figured up some reining-horse prices for a new customer in Italy. He would call him tomorrow. He kept one ear tuned to the hallway, but no one came into the barn except the stable hands to do the morning chores of feeding and stall cleaning.

He went to the house for breakfast, which he ate with his sisters. Only his sisters.

Finally, when ten o'clock rolled around and Cait still hadn't come anywhere near the main barn, the indoor arena, or his office, he went looking for her. Better to lay down the law about the rules for the school before she settled in more deeply and made a bunch of wild-eyed plans that he'd have to put a stop to.

Riding his three-year-old, Sandy, he headed over to the old barn that they used to prevent the spread of any possible infections from outside horses to the Rocking M ones. As he came closer, he saw horses in the runs and two in the old arena, running and kicking in the winter morning breeze. But there was no sign of Cait.

Then he saw her.

She stepped into the open doorway of her trailer, now parked cozily in the lee of the barn in what looked to be a permanent position. Her hair blazed black fire in the sunlight. She wore a dazzling orange turtleneck sweater.

Bright enough to hurt his eyes.

But so becoming to her that it made her easy to look at. More than easy. Impossible to ignore.

She saw him then, and threw up her head to watch him come.

While she went right ahead shaking the hay bag she was emptying out the door.

She was dumping the scraps of leftover hay onto the pile of manure and bedding she'd already swept out of the trailer.

"Don't leave that mess there," he said as he rode up. "First operating rule on the Rocking M is no abuse of animals or people. Second is cleanliness is next to godliness."

Cait looked him over. He was so earnest and so

officious that somehow he reminded her of a little boy. A little boy trying to get control of his world.

He was a grown man, though, and her guess would be that this was the opening shot in a fresh campaign to make her leave the Rocking M. If he couldn't order her off the place, he'd make her want to be gone.

But she wasn't going. She hadn't spent an inordinate amount of money on horses and she wasn't going to do so on rent. She hadn't practically raised herself and lived in poverty all her life to start wasting money now. If she was careful, John's insurance could support this school for a long, long time.

Thank You, Lord, for letting me know that I'm supposed to be here.

She smiled at him.

"I'm sorry, Clint, but I'm leaving it all right where it is. I'm planning to grow mushrooms."

He kept his firmly serious expression the same, but she thought she saw a flash of surprise in his eyes. Then it was annoyance.

"Don't be flip with me, Cait."

"I'm not. I'm perfectly serious."

She hung that hay bag on the hook on the inside of the door and went back inside the trailer for another one. When she stepped out again, Clint was still there. He hadn't moved.

"Fine-looking horse you're riding," she said. "How's he bred?"

"He's a Peppy San Badger," he snapped.

"Training him for a cutter?"

"Working cow horse."

"Well, I like his expression," she said, looking the young stallion over carefully. "He'll be a good one for you."

"Right," he said. "Too bad you didn't use that great eye for horses when you bought this bunch of crumbs."

Cait shook the hay bag out while she tried to hold on to her quick temper.

"Clint, that unkindness doesn't become you," she said. "You're usually such a charming conversationalist."

He shifted impatiently in his saddle.

"Look, Cait, we need to get some things straight."

She hung up that hay bag, too, then met his level gray gaze with a careless one of her own.

"Do you realize you made a rhyme?"

He ignored that, but it distracted him.

"You should've bought your horses from me," he said, although she knew it wasn't what he'd started out to say. "I'd have given you much more value for your money."

Her anger rose.

"You'd have given me the *gate*," she snapped. "And you know it. Besides, I don't need you telling me how to run my business."

"Well, that's exactly what I *am* doing," he said. "If you think you want to hold this school on the Rocking M, then you're going to have to follow some rules."

"No abuse," she said, ticking it off on one finger, "and no messy mushroom patches."

She ticked that one off, too, and raised her eyebrows at him.

"Anything else?"

"Keep your students out of the indoor," he said.

"I've told you a dozen times I'm using this arena," she said firmly.

He held up one hand to stop her right there.

"I mean *out*. Of the whole facility. I don't want hair ribbons and street shoes and clothes scattered all over that bathroom in there," he said. "And no using the shower, either."

"*What?*"

"They can come dressed in their breeches and boots," he said, "and they can leave in them. Have whatever drinks you want for them in a cooler or tell them to bring their own. I don't want them going up to the house, either. Not even if one of them has a grandmother who's my mother's best friend."

She widened her eyes trying to keep her expression sober. Truly, she ought not to let him make these wild assumptions about her students. But she would. It would serve him right.

"All right," she said sweetly. "But which bathroom *can* we use? If there's an urgent need, I mean."

He hadn't thought about that, she could tell.

"I could rent a Porta Potti," she offered, glancing around thoughtfully as if looking for a place to put it. "But you might think it'd ruin the looks of the ranch."

That irritated him thoroughly.

"In the main barn," he snapped. "Either the one next to the breeding lab or the one in the apartment. Nobody's living there right now."

"All right. Anything else?"

"No horseplay, no chattering and giggling near where the trainers are working, no using the phones, no bored mothers hanging out in the customers' lounge waiting for their little darlings."

Cait tried not to laugh. It was almost cruel of her to let him in for the shock that was coming to him, but with his rotten attitude, he deserved it.

"The one rule that bothers me is 'no horseplay,'" she said, smiling. "Sometimes I let them play tag on horseback."

"Don't try to be funny," he snapped. "You know what I mean."

He spoke so scornfully that it killed her smile and any desire to laugh.

"I do know what you mean," she said. "You mean to stay on my case every minute of every day and try to make my life so miserable that I'll either move my school or give it up."

He stared at her, hard. "You got it."

"Give it your best shot."

"I will."

She stared back at him. "I'm staying."

"I doubt it."

And still, neither of them could break the look.

She fell right into his deep gray eyes. For two heartbeats. Or more.

And in that short time—which also seemed incredibly long—something changed between them. Their anger shaded into annoyance, their intensity shifted from fury to searching. Or interest. Or trying to read each other's mind.

No, it was acknowledgment. They both silently admitted, in that one long look, the existence of something else between them. Something that wasn't anger at all.

Even then their gazes held fixed on each other, locked. Neither of them could break away.

Finally Clint scowled even harder, tore his gaze from hers, swung his horse's head around and rode away.

By noon the next day Clint had done more work and accomplished more toward his big projects than he would ever have thought possible. That morning alone he'd made three international phone calls and four long-distance ones that he'd been putting off, he'd written five e-mails to broodmare owners, researched two kinds of new forage for the farm side and bought a new bull from somebody in California.

He made a note about that and got up to go put it on his office manager's desk out in the main office. Dorene would be back at work tomorrow, and that'd be soon enough to make arrangements for shipping the bull.

As he laid the paper down and picked up a paperweight, he heard a low, rumbling roar—a motor, apparently. Coming fast, from the sound of it. Different noise from a diesel truck, though.

It roared right up to the corner, and by the time Clint got to the window the noisy vehicle was wheeling in to park in one of the slots in front of the office, which was in the middle of the long stone barn. In the particular slot he always used when he drove over from the house.

Clint strode to the door and jerked it open.

A lowered pickup truck, the vehicle was mostly primered and ten years old, but equipped with glass pack dual exhausts and a motor so powerful that the whole thing shook as it sat there in his parking place. The driver shut it down and loud, loud music filled the air.

The door of the truck opened and he got out. A kid, barely old enough to drive, from the looks of him. A kid with those sloppy, baggy jeans riding way down on his hips and hair sticking straight up— hair bleached to a shade of whitish yellow that never existed in nature.

Manuel wouldn't have hired somebody like this for his crew. He couldn't be a prospective customer. This kid had to be lost.

Clint walked toward him.

"Can I help you?"

The kid stopped, leaned against the fender of his truck and fingered his hair to see whether it was still sufficiently spiked.

"That depends," he said slowly.

"On what?"

The kid shrugged. His skin was a dark olive, and that made the hair color look even more ludicrous.

"On who you are, man. And what you know."

He smirked as if that were an extremely clever thing to say.

Clint clenched his jaw.

"Where were you headed when you left town? Did you know where you were going?"

The boy looked insulted.

"No *doubt*," he said sarcastically.

Clint gritted his teeth.

"Then where *were* you headed?"

"The ranch."

"Which one?"

Clint snapped the words out. This kid wasn't stupid—he could see the sharp glint of intelligence in his brown eyes.

"The *Rockin'* M."

The boy made a rocking motion with one hand.

"Tight name, man. Like somethin' out of the fifties or somethin'."

He frowned worriedly.

"You know? Like rock 'n roll?"

Then he grinned and Clint saw the sarcasm glinting again.

"You alive in the fifties, man?"

The kid thought that was so funny he could hardly keep from smiling. He managed to keep a straight face, though.

Clint gave him his hardest stare.

"Why the Rocking M?"

"Horses," the boy said. "Hosses. Cowboyin'."

Still leaning against the fender of his truck, he twirled an imaginary rope in the air.

Clint's thin patience snapped.

"You're in the wrong place," he said. "Better hit the road."

The kid waggled his eyebrows and Clint noticed they were bleached to match his hair.

"Not accordin' to the sign, I ain't," he said. "I kin read."

Street kids or skaters or whatever this punk was didn't normally roam this far out of town. There had to be a reason.

"Somebody in particular you're supposed to see out here?"

"Hmm."

The boy glanced at himself in the rearview mirror of his pickup.

"Ya *think*," he said sarcastically.

Clint restrained the urge to close the gap between them, grab him by his thin shoulders and shake him.

"Who is it?" Clint roared.

The kid looked up at him quickly, surprised that Clint was angry.

"McMahan. Miz McMahan."

"Bobbie Ann?"

Bobbie Ann had totally lost her mind. Had she seen this kid in town somewhere and listened to a sob story?

"Is Mrs. McMahan hiring you for some odd jobs or something?"

"Nope. I don't want t' *work,*" the kid said with a grin. "I'm lookin' for Cait."

"*Cait?*"

A relative? But this kid didn't talk like a Chicagoan, and a quick glance showed the pickup had Texas plates.

"You know her? Chick with black hair? Tall? Long legs and…"

The boy stood up straight for the first time and used both hands to outline a feminine body in the air as he stepped away from the pickup.

"I *know* her," Clint said.

A protective urge stabbed through him. This kid had no business even *noticing* Cait, much less coming to see her. He narrowed his eyes and glared at the kid.

"What's your name?"

He walked toward him.

"Joey."

"Well, Joey, you'd better hit the road like I told you. You're way too young for Miss Cait."

Joey didn't back up.

"Na really," he said sarcastically. "Well, *you're* way too old for her, man. I'm *s'posed* to be younger. She's my teacher."

Clint froze in his tracks.

"You're here for the riding school."

It was a statement, not a question, but the disbelief in his voice rang in his own ears.

"Bingo."

It took a couple of moments before Clint could process the information.

"Cait invited you to be a student in her riding school."

"Right," Joey said sarcastically. "How many times I gotta tell you?"

"How did…how did you and Cait meet?"

"My parole officer, if it's any of your business, old man," Joey said. "He's the one hooked us up."

Chapter Six

Cait dropped both the bridles she was hanging on the wall when Clint burst into the tack room behind her.

"Have you lost your mind? What d'you think you're doing bringing a bunch of juvenile delinquents onto this ranch?"

She whirled to face him. He was in a towering rage that made him seem so huge he filled the little room.

"Answer me!"

"Stop shouting and I will!"

He advanced on her. She took a step back, in spite of herself.

Oh, *why* had she thought it'd be funny to let him find out on his own?

"This had better be good, Cait."

His voice changed suddenly, a calm and commanding voice that made her feel cold inside.

What had she done? Had her little joke destroyed the school in one fell swoop?

No! She wouldn't let it!

She took another step back as he kept coming.

"How'd you find out?" she asked, playing for time to think.

"One of your boys drove his low rider up to the office," he said as her shoulders touched the wall.

She leaned back, grateful for the support. She had to pull herself together and *handle* this.

"Looking for Cait," Clint said sarcastically. "'Chick with black hair,' is the way he put it. 'Tall. Long legs...' Well, you get the picture."

He slammed his palms against the wall on either side of her, hemming her in with his arms and his big body. His smoky-gray eyes burned her.

They took the air from her lungs, too.

"Wh-o...who is it?"

She could hardly get enough breath to speak, yet she added desperately, "They're just kids. Not one is really bad."

He ignored that.

"It's Joey," he snapped. "What difference does it make if they're all punks?"

"Well," she said sassily, "you didn't like the idea of spoiled little rich girls."

He leaned even closer, fresh anger snapping in his eyes.

"At least you could've told me the truth."

She lifted her chin.

"At least you could've asked me."

They stood there, glaring. He was so close she could feel his warm breath on her face.

"Joey needs the horses," she said.

The words came out unevenly. She made herself breathe before she went on.

"They all do. And this is their only way to lay hands on them—ever."

"Joey's here for you, not the horses."

She shook her head. Her whole chest constricted. He was so close.

So close it seemed they must be about to touch.

His breath carried the scent of coffee. And cedar.

Her kids. John's memorial. She had to keep her mind on those things instead of thinking of Clint.

"Joey's crazy about horses," she said. "They can keep him out of trouble from now on."

"He *is* trouble."

She shook her head as her natural sassiness came flooding back.

"That's unfair," she snapped. "All he needs is a chance."

Clint snapped right back at her.

"All he needs is a *keeper.*"

The words sounded so flat, so positive, that it scared her even more. What if Clint wouldn't listen to her? Joey and the others *had* to have this chance.

"Clint," she said, searching his face, "help me help these kids. They'll be the *real* memorial to John."

"John's gone. The ranch is still here. I'm the one

responsible for it, and I'm not having a bunch of punks hanging out here all the time.''

"It won't *be* all the time. Only a couple of hours a day for a few days a week.''

"A couple of hours is plenty long enough for trouble. This kid could be a gang member....''

"He isn't,'' she said quickly. "They're not in gangs. Not one of them has been in trouble for anything violent, and I took only the ones who seriously like horses, Clint.''

"How do you know they do?''

"I've had them over to Roy's. I've taken them trail riding. I've spent time with them one on one.''

He shook his head. Instead of anger, his eyes showed pity, as if he were concerned for her sanity.

"Cait, that doesn't mean you know them,'' he said hopelessly.

"I know enough.''

And then, thinking of her students and their bleak lives, she blurted, "I know them because I used to be one of them.''

Clint went very still. He fixed his gaze on her. He was listening.

Cait bit her lip.

She wasn't going to say any more. She never spoke about her past—except she *had* talked about it to John, but she wasn't going to share it with anyone else.

But Clint's reaction gave her the strangest feeling. His storm-gray eyes bored into hers.

"Talk to me, Cait.''

Something about the way he said it loosened her tongue against her will.

He wasn't going to scorn her, whatever she said. Somehow she knew that. Somehow, too, she knew that he sincerely wanted to know.

"I loved horses from the time I knew what one was," she said slowly. "But if we hadn't had a neighbor who galloped horses at the track, I would never, ever have been able to even *touch* a real one."

He waited for more.

Shocked that she was sharing such a private feeling, she went right on talking anyway.

"The first time I laid my hand on a horse, I felt such a peace," she said. "I can't tell you. Beneath my palm was a warm, flesh-and-blood being that would share its sweet spirit with me."

He grinned.

"What?"

She knew, though, that he wasn't laughing at her.

"I was just thinking of some horses whose spirits aren't so sweet."

She smiled.

"But that one was," she said. "She was a middle-aged palomino mare that they ponied the racehorses on. Her name was Sunny. She loved me and I loved her."

"How old were you?"

"Nine. I was blown away by the *idea* of horses. Every single one of them. They were so much bigger and stronger than people, yet they did what people told them, they carried people around on their backs, they tried to please, they listened to their handlers."

He nodded.

He understood what she was talking about. Suddenly she felt a connection between them of a completely different kind. A new kind. For the very first time, their minds were in sync, with no tension between them.

Well, at least not the antagonism they usually felt. There was tension of another kind, though. He was standing very close. Close enough to touch.

And he was still listening.

This was her chance. This was her *kids'* chance.

"Think about it, Clint," she said earnestly. "How would you feel if you couldn't ride, couldn't even get up close to a horse? You can't even imagine it. Not only have you had access to them all your life, you've had at least one horse of your very own since before you could walk. Haven't you?"

He looked at her. He wasn't the least bit interested in hearing about himself and his own life, only about hers.

"They surely didn't let you start ponying the Thoroughbreds when you were *nine,*" he said.

"No. But my neighbor let me ride around the stables every day and do some odd jobs, and by the time I was thirteen I had a job on a farm in exchange for lessons and riding privileges. I lived in the barn."

Clint looked shocked.

"Your parents let you move out at thirteen?"

She bit her tongue. Enough. Too much. She had said too much.

"My aunt. My parents were both dead by then."

It was too painful to talk about her parents.

She stood away from the wall and meant to duck under his upraised arm, but he held her where she was by the power of his look. He didn't move.

His heavy-lidded gaze wandered over her face. It drifted to her mouth. And lingered.

The blood stopped moving in her body.

He was going to kiss her. Was he going to kiss her?

She wanted him to, wanted it more than she could ever remember wanting anything.

She prayed he wouldn't.

For if he did, she could not resist him, she knew that. She would kiss him back. And keep on kissing him.

If he kissed her it would be the beginning of a whole lot of trouble, more trouble than either of them had ever faced.

It would be heavenly if he kissed her.

Yet right now, at this moment, it would break her heart.

Her blood began to move again, began to roar in her ears as she started to understand.

If Clint ever kissed her, it must not be out of pity. Kissing her out of pity would be worse, much worse, than his scorn.

They stood there, at an impasse, for a long, long

moment. Then she saw the comprehension come into his eyes and she knew.

When Clint ever kissed her was closer to the truth. He would kiss her someday, because the big trouble was already with them.

Bigger trouble than if they had kissed.

What they'd felt the day before, with him on horseback and her standing in the doorway of her trailer, was still there, stronger, more insistent—yet now it was an undercurrent to a more powerful bond that had just been born between them. One that was even more compelling.

Understanding. Clint understood, by some miracle, exactly how she felt right now, and he would honor her wishes.

If she ever let herself truly think about that, she'd be lost for good.

For an endless time neither of them moved. They could feel the warmth of each other's breaths, they stared into each other's eyes. The trouble was mapped out for them now, but how could they resolve it?

His stormy gray eyes talked to her. They were saying exactly what her eyes were saying to him. The truth.

I don't want to kiss you. I want to kiss you more than anything.

Finally, after a lifetime, he stood back and let her go.

She walked past him, then stopped in the middle of the little tack room, trying to think what it was she was intending to do, where she was intending to go.

Her students. She was trying to start her school today.

"Clint, what did you do with Joey?"

Her voice came out raspy, as if she'd just woken up.

She gathered the courage to turn and look at him without walking back to him. Stay away. She had to stay away from him for a little while, until her pulse stopped beating so fast.

His gaze was fixed on her as if it had never left.

"Told him to move his car and wait for me in the indoor."

She stared at him in surprise.

"The *indoor?* After all your warnings that we should stay out of there?"

"Had to have somebody keep an eye on him," he said gruffly.

"Are you going to let him out now?"

He grinned, a bit sheepishly, then motioned with a nod for her to walk out the door.

"I'll go on over there," he said.

They walked out of the old quarantine barn into the beautiful day and started toward the indoor. If Clint would let her keep her school, this would be a *truly* beautiful day.

"I admire what you're trying to do for these kids, Cait," he said. "But that Joey's got a real attitude. He'll have to have some rules to go by. If he follows them, I'll give him a chance."

Her temper flared, her heart beat faster. Surely he wouldn't try to micromanage a school he didn't even really want.

"This is my deal, Clint. I'm the one responsible. I'll make the rules."

Then she found a more reasonable tone.

"It's my school," she said. "I'll go over the rules with the kids when they're all together."

"When will that be?"

She glanced at her watch.

"They're due about now."

"I can…"

"No," she said quickly. "I want them to get connected with the horses before we start laying down the law."

He flashed her a doubtful look.

"And, Clint, *I* have to be the authority figure, don't you see? If you come in and start taking over, you'll weaken me considerably."

"No fighting," he said harshly. "No stealing. No vandalism."

Cait took a long, deep breath.

"I'll get the message across. But we can't come right out and say those things to them. We need an atmosphere of trust here, Clint. Some of these kids have never had that, and they need a chance to live up to it."

He didn't answer. He just kept walking.

Finally he said, "We'll see."

And then, "How many students have you signed up?"

"Five. That gives me two horses extra, in case one comes up lame or anything."

"Five is plenty," he said. "Don't take any more."

This time it was she who didn't answer.

She couldn't. She was too busy fighting her sharp tongue and the contradictory feelings rioting in her heart.

Clint was being totally unreasonable and overbearing, dictating to her this way.

Clint was being much more reasonable than she would ever have thought possible. She needed to be glad for that. She needed not to antagonize him again.

Not until he became accustomed to her school and her students.

He threw her a sharp look.

"Cait? Don't take any more students and I'll give these five a chance to prove themselves."

More quick, hot resentment charged through her. He was overstepping his bounds. How many students she had was none of his business.

Yet it was. It was his ranch, too, as he'd reminded her in that early morning on Christmas Eve.

And Bobbie Ann would not protect the school—even as John's memorial—to the detriment of the ranch. Five might be enough, five might be all she could teach and keep an eye on at one time.

Five riders would give her two extra horses, and she might need them in case of incompatibility or temporary lameness or any number of reasons. Trying to borrow horses from the ranch might set Clint off again.

Giving five troubled teenagers an opportunity to know horses and to know God would be far better than giving it to no troubled teenagers at all. These kids really did have only one chance, and they needed that chance more than anything.

She had no choice. She had to get along with Clint.

"All right," she said. "Five's enough for this session."

Which was why Cait immediately said no when Shauna Gilstrap, her horse-show friend—and the social worker who had first asked her to volunteer with troubled teenagers—called late that day. In fact, Cait told her an emphatic no.

"We're full, Shaun," she said. "I didn't even get around to individual help today with all five of these kids I already have."

"Kristen's really alone," Shauna said. "Fourteen is too young to be living in a car."

"Give me a break, Shauna. Fourteen is too young to *have* a car."

"It's her aunt's. *She's* twenty and a traveling musician," Shauna said in her most arbitrary voice.

Shauna was fierce as a mama lion when it came to her kids.

So, somehow, in her heart of hearts, Cait wasn't surprised that when Shauna hauled her horse over to ride with her kids the next afternoon, she brought along an extra horse. And Kristen.

As soon as Kristen opened the door of Shauna's truck and got out, Cait felt she'd entered a time warp, that she was looking at herself at that age. Kristen looked her right in the eye, but only for a second.

It was long enough for Cait to see that the look in her eyes was a combination of ages forty and fourteen and that she had a chip of distrust on her shoulder nearly too big to carry around. She didn't smile at all, didn't even try to fake one.

She had blue eyes instead of black and she was quiet and shyly suspicious instead of bold and eager as Cait had been, but her hair was black and curly and her gaze kept wandering to the horses the others were riding, and Cait felt an instant connection, although she tried very hard not to. Kristen murmured something indistinguishable when Shauna introduced them.

"I brought Buster for Kristen to ride," Shauna said quickly. "I don't want her to be any bother for you."

Cait asked Jennifer, one of her two girl students, to introduce Kristen to the others. Then she turned on Shauna.

"Shauna, you are devious beyond belief," she said. "I cannot take another student, so you'll have to take care of her. And don't make any noise about her joining my class where she can hear it."

Cait pivoted and walked away to get back on her horse.

She was *not* going to go back on her word to Clint. She couldn't. If he threw her off the ranch she'd have a terrible time finding another place. It might be the end of her whole memorial to John.

And it would be another reason for Clint to be alone with her, so close to her another time that he might look at her with his gaze so hot it burned her skin. All she had to do was avoid being alone with him and they wouldn't have to find out where that look might lead.

Therefore, she was *not* going to get involved with Kristen.

Shauna did as she'd been told, and Cait focused on Joey and Jennifer and Darren and his twin, Warren, plus Natalie, the girl with the black lipstick. It was a big job to get them all going with tying and grooming their horses and to help them decide whether she should leave them with the mounts they'd ridden the day before or switch them around.

Even with all that going on, though, she couldn't help but notice that Kristen was having a wonderful time, although she was hardly talking at all. She was listening to Shauna and concentrating on what she was doing and she was patting Shauna's big old roping horse, Buster, but Cait saw that Kristen also was watching everybody else.

Amazingly enough, she even exchanged a few words with Joey when they rode side by side for a little while. Cait caught a glimpse of a smile on

Kristen's lips at something Joey had said. It changed her whole face.

The girl probably had very little to smile about. Maybe she didn't have many friends, if any, at school, since she and her aunt were traveling around. She probably hadn't…

Lord, please help me stop this. Help me think about the good of the five I already have here. Please help me keep my word to Clint.

They were all circling the pen at a slow jog when darkness fell. Everybody had gotten over any fears of riding faster than at a walk.

"Time to go in," Cait called after she'd let them ride until the last possible second. "We have lights in the barn, but none in the pen. Let's put these nice horses to bed."

Shauna and Kristen stayed for that lesson, too, and when it was done and Cait passed out sodas from the old refrigerator in the feed room, they sat around in the aisle on hay bales with the others to rehash everything. Kristen still wasn't talking, but she leaned back against the stall behind her and drank her soda looking much more comfortable than she had when she arrived.

To Cait's delight, the other five were already forming a group, joking and teasing each other about their rides. They really liked this. Clint wouldn't have to worry about their behavior and she probably wouldn't have to give them a single word of warning, because they wouldn't want to lose their new-found fun.

Cait's heart filled almost to bursting.

Thank You, Lord. I am so happy that this is going to work out. I'm going to love this so much, and so are they. They're going to learn about Your love.

She must have closed her eyes for a second while she said the prayer, because when she looked around again and glanced down the aisle of the barn, there was Clint, leaning against the doorjamb, standing in the shadows where he could see the circle of kids.

Her breath stopped. His head was cocked to one side and he was watching and listening carefully. Would he notice there were six kids here instead of five?

She turned her attention back to them. No problem. Kristen wasn't her student.

"I can't remember everything at once," Jennifer was saying, so involved in the horses that all the usual sullenness was gone from her face. "Sit up like a rod is down your spine, square your shoulders, hold your reins even, keep your heels down..."

"Next time, just keep watching me," Joey said. "I've got it in a lock."

A chorus of derision rose, with criticism flying from every direction, but it was all laced with good-will and laughter. Really, it was miraculous that she'd found five kids who could get along like this. Well, six, actually. Kristen was laughing, too.

Natalie said, "You don't have a clue about your own ride, Joey. You were too busy watching Kristen."

Kristen turned bright red and stared at the floor.

Joey grinned.

"Na *really*," he drawled. "And she don't wear no black lipstick."

Natalie bristled and the two of them began to insult each other heartily. Cait sighed. Maybe they weren't going to get along as well as she thought.

"Kristen did so well because *I* was her teacher," Shauna said, throwing a glance at Cait.

Cait pretended to take offense.

"I had five students to your one," Cait said. "And mine all did perfectly great jobs tonight, too."

That little competition distracted Joey and Natalie. Everyone laughed and started reliving their rides again and it was all going to be fine and Cait had only five good students and she was going to have no trouble, really, keeping her word to Clint.

Until Shauna got up to leave and Kristen did, too.

"We're gonna play horseback tag next time," Joey said. "You're on my team, Kristen. We're the Raiders."

Kristen turned and stared at him, wide-eyed. A faint blush tinged her cheeks, but her shyness was forgotten in the rush of shock, then suspicion, then pure happiness that came into her face.

"Thanks, Joey," she said with a smile that would light up Chicago.

He grinned back at her.

She shook her fist in the air. "Raiders win," she said.

All the good-natured teasing started again.

Cait stood transfixed, held perfectly still by her

fast-beating heart that felt both too light and too heavy.

It was too late now.

She wouldn't say anything to Clint about it tonight, though. They'd hash this out later. For one night, at least, she'd bask in the memory of that smile lighting up Kristen's thin face.

She introduced Clint to everyone as they drifted out of the barn to their assorted vehicles, and then they made small talk as she went around checking everything one last time and turning out the lights.

"That Joey's a natural horseman," she said, hoping to get Clint started on his usual tirade about Joey's dress and behavior instead of the number of teenagers there tonight. "He may be ready to sign up for some of the smaller shows this summer."

"He might," Clint said, walking with her out to her truck, parked in the glow of the security light. "You seem to have several in the bunch who like to show off."

"And several who really like horses, don't you agree?"

He looked down at her for a long minute, but she couldn't read his eyes in the shadow of his hat.

A knot formed in her chest. Surely, *surely,* if he were going to challenge her on the head count, he would've already done it.

"I do agree," he said with a nod. "Looks like you've picked some good ones—kids *and* horses."

Shocked by his mellowness, she waited. He was bound to challenge her about Kristen now.

But he didn't.

He waited for her to speak.

She didn't.

Her only comfort was that she hadn't actually *promised* Clint. She had not used the word *promise* anywhere in that conversation.

She tilted her head and looked him in the eye as she gave him a great big smile.

He smiled back, then took off his hat and popped it against his thigh.

"Well, Cait," he drawled, "I'm headed for the house. It's been a long day, hasn't it?"

"You could say that," she said.

Their gazes clung. They couldn't stop smiling.

"See you tomorrow," he said.

She nodded.

"Be careful," he said.

Was he talking about her school? He had read her mind about Kristen—she knew it as well as she knew he still wanted to kiss her.

"I will," she said, her smile widening to a grin. "You, too."

"Always," he said.

Then he turned and walked jauntily off down the hill, whistling softly to himself. He popped his hat against his thigh one more time.

"So," Cait murmured to herself, unable to stop smiling, "let the games begin."

Chapter Seven

Clint was thinking about Christmas as he drove his pickup out of the circle drive in the dark early the next morning. Ironic facts—Christmas was here and he wanted it to go away, Christmas was gone and he wanted…

What he really wanted, he had to admit, was to see Cait. To talk to Cait.

To kiss Cait.

He'd been wanting that as a thirsty man wanted water ever since he'd come so close. He'd been dreaming about it all night.

Truth to tell, he'd been dreaming about it since he woke up, too.

That was why he was thinking about Christmas right now. He was remembering how she'd looked that night in silk and velvet.

Even more dangerous, though, he was remembering how she'd looked at *him* when he'd left her at the barn with her *six* kids having departed. And worse than that was the way he'd felt, walking down the hill, whistling.

Like a kid, for heaven's sake, a kid caught up in the excitement of the challenge, the thrill of the game. He'd had no one to play with until Cait came. He'd felt like a teenager himself, buoyed by the twinkle in her eyes and the understanding, that mysterious understanding that kept leaping to life between them. She was going to add that new girl to the rest of her brood and she knew that he knew it. She'd told him that with one bright, teasing look and he'd taken the challenge to see what fun there was to come.

He had to stop this. It would be a huge mess if he started something with Cait.

He set his jaw. She was only twenty years old, for heaven's sake, and, God help him, she was his own brother's wife.

God, help me. Please.

That was the first prayer he'd said, even silently, since Jackson's wreck. He hadn't been too friendly with God lately, what with the huge load of grief and frustration he was carrying, but surely God would help him with this one thing.

Bobbie Ann might've been right. Maybe he should make a trip to the chapel. Just as soon as he had the time.

Just as soon as he had the nerve to go and get on his knees over something that he should be able to handle for himself.

Starting now, starting this minute, he was going to stay away from Cait, and when he couldn't avoid her, he would treat her like a friend. An acquaintance.

Why, he never knew what her reaction might be to anything he said. He was not going to lose control of his senses over a young woman who was always making fun of him with her quick remarks, who, with no warning at all, could turn hot or cold, flip or serious—or inexplicably trusting.

That had amazed him when she'd told him those bits about her past.

Which had set him to imagining what Christmas must have been like for her when she was thirteen and living in somebody's barn. He clamped his mind shut on that image.

He would remain in control of his own mind and his own emotions just as he would remain in control of this ranch. He was going to stop thinking about Cait as of this minute.

Clint shook his head to clear it and took another sip of strong coffee from the insulated mug. Maybe he should get out more. His secret vice evidently wasn't enough distraction.

If he was so desperate for entertainment that Cait's story fascinated him, he ought to start playing checkers with the old men in the back room at Hugo's or take up hitching horsehair or knitting. He wheeled the truck out onto the road with one hand as he took another drink of coffee.

Midnight would wake him up and help him get his head on straight. That colt never failed him.

After he parked the truck in front of the office, he finished the coffee in one gulp and opened the door. The morning was warm, too warm for December, so he stepped out, peeled off his jean jacket and threw it into the back seat.

As he slammed the door, he heard a horse squeal. The two sounds merged, so he stood still and listened again.

Sure enough, a loud, rolling call sounded, apparently from one of the young studs in show training. It hadn't come from the stud barn—it was from inside the main barn, or maybe from one of the runs behind it. Some of the stalls probably had been left open to the outside during this warm, muggy night.

He went through the office and jerked open the door to the center aisle that ran the whole length of the barn. The main doors on each end of it stood open and so did the back doors of some of the stalls.

The squeals were louder now. Definitely two different horses, and they were outside. Plus Midnight and a couple of others who were inside joining in the racket.

Clint started down the aisle, looking through to the outside runs.

At Trader's stall he stopped and reached for the latch. The horse was outside and another one was with him. Impossible.

Surely not.

Clint blinked and looked again. The security

lights, high on the poles behind the barn, reflected off Trader's black hide as he reared and squealed again.

And bred a mare that looked like melted gold against the dark night.

Too late. He was too late.

Clint grabbed for the halter and lead rope anyway, jerked them off the front of the stall door and started through the stall to the run, his mind racing. What palomino mare was on the place? Who was this? How'd she get here?

So as not to startle the horse, he stopped in the doorway and waited for Trader to see him. Finally he did, and finally he came to him. He let Clint lead him into the stall with only his arm around his neck.

Clint fastened him in, then turned to the mare. The yellow horse was standing watching him and he stared at her in disbelief. His eyes were not deceiving him. This wasn't a strange palomino. It was that ugly buckskin mare of Cait's.

He turned to look toward the quarantine barn on the hill as if he could see through the dark to trace the path she'd taken to get to this one. His jaw tightened. Cait's kids had better learn to close a gate and a stall, and make sure they were fastened.

That was the first thing a person should know about life on a ranch—never, ever leave a gate open that should be closed. All kinds of destruction could result from the wrong animals being thrown together, and tonight was a prime example.

The mare looked at him with a baleful eye as he

passed her to close the back gate that was swinging open. It could have been open for hours. During that time Trader could've gone anywhere on the ranch, gotten into any kind of trouble. He could have broken a leg and had to be put down.

An unreceptive mare could've kicked him and broken his leg.

Surely none of Manuel's crew had been so careless.

And surely Cait hadn't let any of her kids come down here.

Maybe she'd given them a tour of the facility and hadn't been able to watch all of them at once. Had that kid Joey resented Clint enough to do something like this on purpose?

Likely not. He'd been too wrapped up in the new girl, who looked a little like Cait, to be thinking of mischief.

He'd talk to Manuel and his men the minute they showed up to work.

Clint closed the gate, then walked toward the mare with the halter in his hand. She waited until the last minute, turned her head and ducked away, darted to the opposite corner of the run. It took him three more tries to catch and halter her.

"There's nothing that irritates me like a horse that won't be caught," he told her as he buckled the halter. "You're about to get tied up for a while."

The mare called to Trader again and he called back.

Clint turned and led her out the back gate of the

run, locking it carefully behind him. Then he took her across the road to one of the saddling bays in the indoor arena and cross-tied her.

Only then, with both horses taken care of, did he let himself think about the razzing he'd get if Trader's first foal turned out to have a big, ugly head and a disposition to match. Despite all his determination to stay away, he would have to go see Cait today.

Cait was trying to hum along with the radio as she turned out of Roy's ranch road onto the two-lane highway. She couldn't carry the tune, though, because she couldn't concentrate enough to even know what it was. All she could think about was whether she'd see Clint at the Rocking M today or not.

She'd been looking forward to it all day, as hard as she'd tried not to think about it. They'd started something last night.

Not just the silent understanding, not just the near kiss, but the teasing. He knew she was keeping Kristen and he knew she knew he knew it.

And she knew he was going to make her pay. That look he'd given her and that slap of his hat on his leg had been a promise of retribution.

With a mischievous smile on his sensuous lips.

Lord, please give me the strength to stay away from him. And please fill my mind with other things besides him.

He might not be there today, and it'd be best if

he wasn't. She would stay right at her barn, stay busy every minute, and keep her kids close around her the whole time.

Maybe Clint would stay at the house. Or in his famous indoor arena. Anywhere but at her barn.

Their paths were certain to cross sometimes, though. When they did, she was going to stay away from anything the least bit personal. She would be pleasant, but she would be brief and businesslike.

She would literally stay away from him every minute that she could.

The way she felt about Clint—this connection with him—just made her feel so *guilty*. It was a betrayal of John. What was she doing, trying to build a living memorial to John's memory and John's faith when she was obsessing over John's brother?

The thought had worn a rut in her mind. Stubbornly she banished it and forced herself to focus on something else—on her work.

Cait had had years and years of practice at putting her worries away for another day and refusing to think about anything that bothered her. By the time she wheeled her truck into the arched entrance that had Rocking M Ranch written in big, fancy, iron script overhead, she was singing with the radio and going over every detail of her ride that morning on Overtime, her problem colt. He wasn't a bad mover—he just had a bad attitude, really bad, but today he'd been good. Today had been their best ride yet.

Just recalling it made her smile. Patience. That was all she needed, patience and a lot of listening to that horse, and she'd get him shown. Roy had told her he doubted anybody could do it.

Cait smiled to herself. Roy was a generous and fair boss who was good to sing her praises when she deserved it. If she could show that horse well and place on him most of the time, it'd help build her name for that faraway day when she went out on her own.

She drove by Clint's precious, off-limits-to-her-kids indoor arena and was passing the end of the main barn when he, himself, stepped out of the shade of the doorway. Without so much as a thought, she stopped.

Without so much as a word, he opened the passenger door and got in.

As if he'd been waiting for her.

As if it were the most natural thing in the world for her to stop and pick him up.

Cait shifted the gears and set the truck in motion again, turned the corner to head up toward ''her'' barn.

As if they went somewhere together every day of their lives.

''What's going on?'' she said.

He shrugged.

''Oh, not much. Mostly sittin' around the office with my feet up, thinkin' about you.''

Her heart racketed suddenly in her chest. She

slowed carefully for a depression in the gravel road, then risked a glance at him.

He was giving her a look, and it was flirtatious, but there was more to it. It had a mischief in it as strong as when he left her last night.

Let the games begin.

She held his gaze and gave him a slanting smile of her own.

"And what, exactly, were you thinking about me?"

"Oh," he said, with elaborate casualness, "just wonderin' if you know how to count, that's all."

She let out a breath she didn't know she'd been holding.

"Yep," she said, "and I counted an extra blessing yesterday. We're gonna do just fine."

"Not unless all six of 'em learn to close a gate."

Now he was utterly serious.

Cait gripped the wheel tighter and the truck swerved.

"All right, tell me. What happened?"

"Trader gave your mare a free breeding last night."

She stared at him harder. He wasn't teasing, but there was still some humor in his eyes. She tried to encourage it.

"Hey, thanks," she said. "That's something I couldn't afford on my own."

"I'd like to say you're welcome," he said wryly. "But we didn't go *get* her. She came to us."

She searched his face.

"I can tell you're ticked off," she said, "but not upset to the point of being your usual fire-breathing self. Which mare?"

His frown gave her the answer.

"That ugly buckskin one that won't let you catch her," he said in an aggrieved tone.

"Don't take it personally," she said. "Daisy's lazy. She's afraid if you catch her, she'll have to work."

"She will, if I ever get hold of her again."

They reached the barn and Cait pulled in and parked beside her trailer.

"Anyhow, teach your kids to fasten a gate, won't you, Cait?"

"I did! I do! How come you're picking on us? There're a hundred people around here every day."

"They're old hands. They don't make that kind of mistake."

"Everybody makes *every* kind of mistake," she said as she threw the truck into Park and turned off the motor.

"The last thing we need is for Trader's first foal to be out of that ugly mare. It'd be a laughingstock."

She stiffened.

"And how do you know that?" she said stubbornly. "Children can be better looking than both their parents put together."

He narrowed his eyes at her, as if to say she knew better than that.

"*And* vice versa," she said significantly, looking him up and down.

"This is no time for jokes."

"That's not a joke."

She waited a beat.

"More of an observation."

He nearly grinned, but he controlled it.

"I'll tell Bobbie Ann you said that," he said. "I'm not sure if she'll defend my looks or thank you for the compliment to herself."

The cab of the truck felt very small with Clint in it—he'd filled it right up since the moment he got in. He turned to face her, with one long leg bent. His knee touched hers. She had turned to face him, too.

She ought to open the door and get out now, but she couldn't bear to move away from the heat of his touch.

"Clint, this was an accident. It could've happened to anyone."

She looked at him and grinned.

"I know you're not open to blackmail," she said. "I, however, am entirely vulnerable to bribery. You could make me an offer to keep the sire's name secret when Daisy foals."

His good humor faded as he visualized the possibilities. He scowled at her.

"*If* she foals," he snapped. "Maybe she won't."

"Right," she said. "If. Where was Trader? Did he jump a fence to get to her?"

"Nope. She was in his run when I got to the barn this morning."

Suddenly they both seriously thought about that.

"Gate open?" Cait said.

"Right. At the end of the run."

Cait stared at him.

"Then how can you blame us? None of us was anywhere near your barn."

"What about after they left you?"

"Well, I didn't watch every vehicle leave the ranch with my own eyes, but they were all tired from riding and it was really late when we finished."

"When Manuel's man brought your mare back up here, her stall was standing open, too."

Cait puzzled over it.

"It makes no sense. Manuel's crew are the only people who'd have reason to be at both barns."

"I talked to him. He doesn't have anybody that green on the crew and nobody that careless."

The sun was coming in through the open window and warming the work-weary muscles in her back and shoulders. The breeze was light, mild and it smelled vaguely of spring.

She didn't want to move. Ever again.

But suddenly Clint sat up and stared over her shoulder.

"Your twins," he said.

Cait turned. Darren and Warren were coming out of the barn, each holding a longe line and whip, each leading the horse he'd ridden before, the four of them plodding along in single file, headed for the old arena.

"I had no idea they were in there," she said. "Where's their vehicle?"

She called to them.

"Darren and Warren! How'd you get here?"

They stopped, turned and stared.

"Our uncle dropped us off," Warren called back.

"On his way to Mexico," Darren added.

Then they went on about their business as if they knew exactly what they were doing.

"Mexico," Clint murmured thoughtfully, teasing her. "I wonder when he plans to pick them up."

"I wonder *if* he plans to pick them up," Cait said. "If he's in that old gray van they were driving yesterday, I don't think he has much hope of getting *back* from Mexico."

They watched while the boys led their horses into the pen and carefully closed the gate behind them. Then they walked to opposite ends and stopped, ready to begin.

Warren's horse refused to move. The boy shook the longe line, waved the whip, yelled and stomped his feet. Nothing worked. All four feet could have been nailed to the ground.

Darren's horse ambled in a wider and wider circle that soon drew Darren farther and farther from the spot he had picked to stand. He couldn't seem to coax any gait faster than the same slow walk out of his mount.

"Do you know why I think those two got in trouble in the first place?" Cait said lazily.

"I feel sure you're about to tell me," Clint said in the same tone.

"Because their names don't rhyme. I'm thinking their mother thought they did, but they don't. That'd be very discouraging for twins—names that look alike but don't rhyme."

Clint grinned. Really wider than she'd expected.

"Cait," he said, reaching to brush back a curl from her forehead, "I think you're onto something there. But right now we better get between the twins and *future* trouble. One's in danger of being dragged to death by a runaway horse and the other could petrify in place."

Cait's heart suddenly beat faster. *We.*

They reached to open their doors at the same time.

Clint was going to *help* her with her kids.

Clint drove his dually into Jackson's yard—Jackson and *Darcy's* yard—turned it around and backed up to the wood rack. By the time he'd shut off the motor and got out, Jackson was coming from the barn.

"Well," he called. "It's the man Clint, himself. What happened? You finally get so cranky all your help quit you?"

"Takes one to know one," Clint called back, reaching to his hip pocket for his gloves. "Must be your sunshiny personality that makes me so eager to haul your wood for you."

Jackson frowned at him, but it was only a pale imitation of his old scowl. These days, Jackson couldn't stop smiling long enough to really get crossways about anything.

"Darcy says we're wasting our time," he said as he got closer. "She says with the weather this hot we'd accomplish more by hauling ice to the water tanks."

"Smart woman," Clint said. "She's nailed it."

"She's always thinking about the animals," Jackson said. "It's the veterinarian in her."

Clint grinned.

"What?" Jackson said as he pulled out his own gloves and started pulling them on.

The sight warmed Clint through and through. Until Darcy came along, Jackson had worn gloves constantly to conceal his hands. They had been badly burned in the truck wreck that had crushed his leg.

"*What* are you grinning at?" Jackson demanded.

"You," Clint said, and picked up the first sticks of wood from the truck. "The brand-new Jackson, proud as a peacock of his veterinarian woman."

Jackson grinned back.

"You nailed it," he said.

"And after that baby's born you'll be even worse," Clint said.

"Yep."

Jackson filled his arms with wood and stacked it neatly onto the rack.

Clint followed with another load. Once he had it stacked, he straightened and looked at his brother.

"How's it going to change you, Jackson? First a

wife, now a child. How d'you think you'll be different after that?''

Surprised, Jackson stopped at the back of the truck and turned to look at him.

Clint waited, suddenly tense with the need to know, helpless to imagine what it would be like to be a husband, much less a father.

''I can't say about the baby,'' Jackson said thoughtfully. ''But being a husband is a new gift every day. I still can't believe anybody could love me that much.''

Such a gentle trust reposed in his brother's weathered face, such a happiness now lived in his blue eyes that had shown nothing but bitterness for so long, that Clint couldn't look away.

A flash of loneliness shot through him. A lightning strike of unutterable solitude that hollowed him out inside.

Would anybody ever love him in that way? And could it be that he would love her in return as much as Jackson loved Darcy?

Jackson seemed to read his mind.

''Sorry,'' he said. ''I'm no good with words. But does that help you any?''

Defensively Clint's heart closed around itself.

''I'm only trying to figure out if you'll be too wrapped up at home to help me out,'' he said quickly.

And that was true. Selfishly true.

''Looks like you're comin' out of your long, dark funk,'' he said. ''So, lovebird or not, you might think about showin' up at the barn every once in a while."

Jackson gave him a long, indulgent look—as if he were the older, wiser brother.

"I'm your man," he said reassuringly. "You can depend on me."

He smiled at Clint, then turned to get another armload of wood. Clint let out his breath, a little at a time.

Jackson was making a family of his own, but he still was a part of the bigger family, too.

Clint went with him to get more wood.

"Just wait till that baby's a teenager," he said. "You should come over and see those kids of Cait's, spiked hair and black lipstick and all."

"When he's a teenager he'll be hanging out with his uncle Clint," Jackson said. "You'll be in charge of discipline and you are *not* to let him wear black lipstick."

"If I'm in charge, I'll make the rules," Clint said. "Don't be trying to dictate to us, Pops."

He kept thinking about that as they worked. Uncle Clint. He kind of liked the sound of that.

Chapter Eight

New Year's Day was another do-as-you-please holiday on the Rocking M, with eating black-eyed peas to ensure an upcoming year of prosperity as the only hard and fast tradition of the day. Which worked out great, because this year Clint and Jackson wanted to watch the football games, Delia wanted to go into Austin to hear a brand-new bluegrass band, LydaAnn wanted to go to a jackpot barrel racing and Bobbie Ann and Darcy wanted to go to a special antique-filled open house at one of the bed-and-breakfast inns in Fredericksburg.

As it turned out, Clint and Jackson were the only McMahans who didn't start the New Year doing exactly what they wanted.

They were completely engrossed in watching the first bowl game of the day, which was unexpectedly close in the middle of the fourth quarter, when

LydaAnn ran through the great room on her way out the back door.

"Heads up, boys. Loose horse," she said.

Then she vanished.

No matter how absorbing *anything* was, those last two words were always guaranteed to grab attention.

Clint tore his gaze from the big screen, turned his head and looked the charming Miss Daisy right in the eye. She lifted her head and touched her muzzle to the glass of the bay window as if to blow him a kiss.

He glanced at Jackson, who was also staring at her in total disbelief.

"What in the world?" he said.

"*Who* is leaving the gates open around here?" Clint demanded.

Then he yelled, "LydaAnn!"

He leapt up and ran to the back door, then out onto the stone patio in his sock feet. His sister was halfway to her truck.

"LydaAnn," he bellowed. "Catch her and put her up. *Please!*"

She turned around and walked backward while she flashed him the charming smile that always helped her get her way.

"I don't even have my boots on," he said.

"I'm not the one who let her out," she yelled back. "Sorry, but I'm already late. Jackson'll help you."

Heartlessly she jumped into her truck and fired it up, pulling away down the driveway with the two-horse trailer containing her best barrel horse and her young barrel-horse-in-training racing along behind her. While Cait's incorrigible buckskin mare trompled Bobbie Ann's bushes and tore up the lawn.

Fine daughter LydaAnn was, and he intended to tell her so. Didn't she even care about her mother's yard?

He forced himself to walk, not run, around the corner of the house. If he could get an arm around that mare's neck, he'd use his belt to hold her until Jackson could bring him a halter.

Daisy saw him coming, though. She backed up slowly, thoroughly trampling everything green she could get her feet on, pinned her ears and snorted at Clint.

He stopped where he was.

"I'm not even going to give you the pleasure of chasing you," he said.

Then he froze. Behind Daisy, far behind her, another loose horse was trotting briskly down the road that ran between the barn and the indoor arena. Another was ambling along the white board fence near the stud barn.

Clint recognized both of them as belonging to Cait.

His blood pressure rose.

Manuel and his crew were having a holiday. They'd be here, but only late in the afternoon to feed and pick stalls again.

He turned and went back inside.

"Jackson," he said. "You'll have to help me."

"Game's nearly over," Jackson said with his eyes glued to the television screen.

Clint watched it, too.

"It's going to go into overtime," he said.

"Maybe she'll just hang out there in the yard for a little while."

Clint stuffed his feet into his boots without even sitting down.

"You're as bad as LydaAnn," he said irritably. "Don't even care if the yard gets trashed."

Jackson glanced at him then.

"There're three of 'em out," Clint said. "Maybe more. We'll have to put them up, like it or not."

Jackson sighed and bent over to reach for his boots, too.

"Rotten luck," he groused.

"Rotten supervision," Clint said, and felt vaguely disloyal to Cait.

From what he'd seen so far, she was keeping a very close eye on her young charges.

"Or rotten carelessness on some student's part."

"The ones out are all Cait's?"

"All that I've seen so far."

They left the room together, both with one last, longing look at the screen.

"If a student's being careless, how do you explain Trader's gate being open the other night?" Jackson said.

"I can't," Clint said. "Coincidence, I guess. Manuel's crew could've made a mistake, too."

They walked quietly up behind Daisy, flanked her

and drove her slowly toward the road up to the quarantine barn. Once, they cornered her against the pasture fence, but she feinted one way and broke the other and Jackson couldn't move fast enough to stop her.

Clint glanced at his brother as the mare darted past him. He appeared to accept the fact that he was no longer fast on his feet. Gloom didn't consume him as it would have in the months before Darcy. Recognizing that fact lessened Clint's own irritation.

He spoke before he thought.

"Too bad Cait's arrival's had the opposite effect of Darcy's," he blurted. "She's created more trouble than she's eased."

Jackson glanced at him sharply.

Clint snapped his mouth shut. What in the world was the matter with him, comparing Cait to Darcy?

"Let's go saddle up," he said. "We've got at least three of them to gather, maybe all seven. And no help."

His frustration rose even higher as they went to get their mounts. He fought it to try to think clearly.

"This is more than a careless kid," he said. "Each one's responsible for his own horse. With several of the horses out, we know somebody did this deliberately."

"Looks that way," Jackson said. "But who? Cait and her kids weren't here last night, 'cause it was New Year's Eve. Manuel fed them this morning and these nags were all in their places then or he'd have told you."

Clint turned and looked at him, hard.

"You're right. I'm jumping to conclusions."

"Might be Grandpa's spirit," Jackson said with a teasing grin. "Trying to teach you to be more open-minded and not to pick on Miss Cait and her kids."

His blue eyes glinted with mischief.

"Reckon Old Clint rides again?"

But even Old Clint, marvelous tenor that he had been, couldn't sing like an angel come to earth. That was Clint's first thought when he walked into the main barn late the next day.

An ethereal voice stopped him in his tracks. A woman's voice, singing about mountains and a horse and the moon. It seemed completely unreal to hear that instead of the usual constantly playing radio, but it was real.

The woman was here in the barn someplace.

It wasn't Delia. Not LydaAnn. Cait? Could Cait sing like that?

No, Cait was up at the other barn. He'd looked for her truck just before he'd come by here to get something from his office.

He walked on in, the strangest feeling passing over him. Here lately, every time he stepped out of the house he ran across something else unexpected. Sometimes unexplainable.

The wandering melody floated toward him on the air and wound itself around his heart. He went toward the sound, glancing from side to side at the quietly resting horses, until he found her.

She was in the stall with Midnight.

Clint's breath caught in his throat. It was the shy, black-haired girl, Cait's last student, in the perfect position to be smashed into the concrete wall if the colt spooked. She was singing to him, scratching his withers and smiling at him, watching his lower lip droop with pleasure.

Even without that, Midnight didn't look like himself. He stood with one hind foot cocked and his eyes half closed, ears slanted back to listen to the song. No wariness, no orneriness, no nervousness.

The dying sunlight slanted through the high window above the west door and lit the girl's face, made her look like a child lost in a make-believe world. All wrapped up in the horse and her song, she was oblivious to Clint's presence.

He stood in silent amazement. How could this be? A city kid, inexperienced with horses, and she had a connection like this with a horse? With *this* horse?

You'd think Midnight was a ten-year-old show horse this girl had been showing all his life instead of a fractious two-year-old barely started. He needed to get her out of there.

But they needed each other a little while longer, these two young creatures who were no strangers to trouble. And it seemed a shame to interrupt the song.

He had to get that ignorant girl out of that stall.

She knew the exact spot where Midnight loved to be scratched.

The next line of the song had a girl on a horse making a break for the border.

The next thing he knew, Midnight would be gone and this girl would be riding him, trying for her own escape.

But still he couldn't move. Her voice held him as mesmerized as the horse seemed to be.

Clint felt, rather than heard, movement behind him and turned to see Cait coming around the corner from the cross-hallway that led to the back door. She stopped in her tracks, as he had done, and took in the scene.

Then she met his gaze and, with a little shrug, held out her open hands as if to say she hadn't known about this, either. Silently she came closer.

He caught her scent, her own light fragrance that smelled of lemons or maybe oranges, and he wanted her to come even closer. He ached to reach out and touch her bare arm.

Foolish, foolish man that he was. What he needed to do was run from her, even if he had to leave all the teenagers she knew in the stalls with his horses.

She watched the girl and Midnight for a minute more, then looked at him with her huge dark eyes full of wonder. To share what she felt, to say she knew he felt it, too.

He did. He felt wonder and he also felt confusion as strong as any he'd ever known, felt them both pouring into his blood and through his bones as his control of the ranch—of his life, actually—was flowing out through his fingers like water through rocks.

Loose horses with no explanation for their freedom. Angels singing at twilight. A two-year-old stud colt acting like a backyard pet.

A stunning, strong and fascinating woman looking at him with wonder in her eyes.

He didn't know what to think about any of that here on the Rocking M, where he was accustomed to knowing everything that was going on and what he should do about every bit of it. He didn't know anything anymore.

Except that Cait had appeared out of nowhere on Christmas Eve and nothing had been the same since.

Cait looked from Kristen's face to Clint's and prayed that he wouldn't get angry. This was a miraculous sight, the strongest miracle she'd seen since Clint had stayed on this colt's back on Christmas Eve.

But she had to get Kristen out of there for now. She had to do it before Clint did, because he'd probably bar the child from the black horse forever.

The line of his jaw hardened and he took a step toward the stall.

The song ended. The last high, haunting notes lingered in the still air.

"I saw you in a dream, Nighthorse," Kristen said quietly. "More than once. On the high mountain ridges. Did you know that was you—the horse in my song?"

The lowering sun slanted in from the west, laying

two strips of light down in the aisle. It touched Kristen's face, too, and showed her completely at peace.

No way could Cait be angry that she'd disobeyed the instruction to go straight to the tack room and come straight back. There was a force at work here that was from God.

Because Kristen was happy. Content. Both emotions were in her face and her voice, in the way she stroked the horse now with reverent hands.

"You've been in my heart for a long time," Kristen told him.

She started toward his head, and Clint took another step, but then he stopped when Kristen hugged the colt around the neck. Not good to startle them now.

Neither noticed that anyone else existed, much less right nearby. The horse was as mesmerized as the girl.

When she let him go, he lifted his gorgeous head, turned and blew at her affectionately, drawing in her scent. Kristen patted his neck lovingly, then began scratching him again.

"Kristen," Cait said softly. "Did you find a martingale?"

The horse and the girl both startled. He jumped sideways, but Kristen didn't panic as some newbies did—she just stepped out of his way and then laid her hand on his back.

"N-n-not yet," she said. "Soon as I came in here, I saw Nighthorse."

Clint spoke softly, too, but Cait heard the tension in his voice.

"I call him Midnight," he said.

Startled again, apparently that he had spoken directly to her, Kristen looked at him and then quickly away, as her shy, closed look returned to her face.

There was something else in his tone, though—almost a kinship of some kind, and Kristen heard it, too. She gathered her nerve and glanced at Clint again.

"So we're not very original, are we?" she said. "Naming a black horse something about night."

"Can't argue with that," Clint said. "Maybe we should think again."

"I couldn't change it," Kristen said. "Nighthorse was the name that came with my dream."

She shot Clint a quick look from her bright blue eyes.

"Did you dream his name was Midnight?"

"No," he said, "it was the first thing that came to my tongue the first time I rode him."

She lifted her face then and looked directly at Clint.

"I want to ride him."

It was a statement and a question and a request, all rolled up into one. Its tone was very sincere—and very firm.

Cait held her breath.

Lord, please don't let him crush her. She's found her horse. Please give her time here to find You, too.

"You might have to wait a while," Clint said kindly. "He's only getting started and he tries to throw everyone who gets on him."

Kristen thought about that while Cait began to breathe again.

"He wouldn't try to throw *me,* though."

Now it was Clint's turn to think about it.

Cait twisted her fingers together.

Lord, please give him patience with this child.

"Well, we don't want to take that chance just yet," he said. "If you got hurt, then you couldn't ride at all, not even your lessons horse."

"Nighthorse would *never* hurt me."

Clint stepped up to the stall door, which wasn't latched.

"He wouldn't *mean* to hurt you," he said. "But horses are prey animals. Do you know what that means?"

Kristen looked away, shook her head slightly to say that she didn't.

"When something scares them and it's time for a fight or flight, they flee. When they panic and run they don't think at all, so he could accidentally hurt you."

She looked at the horse, then back at Clint.

Her shyness with him was lessening. Or she was so desperate in her quest that she'd dare anything.

She actually held Clint's gaze with a steady, earnest one of her own.

"He won't be scared. He's brave, aren't you, Nighthorse?"

She patted the colt again. Clint slowly opened the door of the stall.

"I tell you what," he said. "For now let's leave this colt to think about that song you sang to him and you go find that martingale. All right?"

Kristen responded to the firmness in his voice. Reluctantly she gave the colt a last pat and walked through the door Clint was holding open.

"The tack room's right around that corner," Cait said, pointing her in the right direction. "Then run on back to the other barn and tell everybody I'll be there in a minute, will you, please?"

Kristen left them.

Clint slid the bar into place on Midnight's stall and latched it.

"I was on my way up to talk to you," he said. "Let's go, so the others won't be riding unsupervised."

He didn't sound critical, though, just matter-of-fact.

"Shauna's there."

She waited a beat for emphasis.

"If she hadn't been, I'd have sent another student instead of coming after Kristen myself."

"Sorry," he said mildly. "I should've known."

Thank goodness, for Kristen's sake, he wasn't trying to antagonize her.

"Clint," she said, "about Kristen..."

"What was the deal, sending her down here after a martingale?" he said. "Do you need equipment?"

She stared at him.

"Why? Are you going to buy it for me?"

He shrugged.

"Probably not. But there's tons of tack on this place. We can scare up whatever you need."

"I'm fine. I just needed another martingale. Let me know if you need it back."

He turned and leaned against the stall door, looking at her thoughtfully.

Her breath got a little tight in her chest. She remembered what he'd said.

"What did you want to talk to me about?"

"Your mare got out again. Plus two of the others."

"Mine?"

"Yep. The roan and that rangy sorrel gelding."

Her heart was beating faster. Much faster.

"What's going on here?"

"That's what I want to know. Maybe somebody in your outfit isn't latching the stalls securely."

"When did you find them?"

"Yesterday. Jackson and I missed the end of a bowl game trying to put them up. We finally had to rope your yellow mare."

He still didn't seem angry. Was he getting ready to throw her off the place?

She banished the worry. She had to think.

"We weren't here the night before," she said. "Somebody had to go in and out of the stalls then and again yesterday morning. If we'd left doors undone, the horses would've been out long before your ball game came on."

"That's what Jackson said."

"Well, good for him!"

She flashed a smile.

"I'm training my kids to be responsible, Clint. They're taking good care of their horses and they're *not* leaving stalls unlatched."

He rubbed his hand over his eyes.

"Sometimes I think we've got a ghost," he said. "I can't figure this out."

"I can't, either. What does Manuel say?"

"Swears it's not his crew."

"With everyone aware now, we'll find out pretty soon," she said. "But I hate that somebody's fooling with my horses."

Clint's jaw tightened.

"So do I. I'm responsible for them."

"You can't be everywhere at once in an operation this size," she said soothingly. "You'll know soon enough."

He looked deep into her eyes, just for a moment, as if taking comfort from her. Then he was all business again.

"And now this thing with the shy girl and the black colt," he said.

Her stomach clutched.

"You did a really good job of handling that situation," she said quickly. "Thanks for being so understanding with her."

"She has to stay away from him."

The knot in the center of her body tightened even more.

"But Clint, think about it...."

"If you don't want to tell her, I will."

"Kristen's made a real connection with that colt," Cait said, talking fast so he couldn't say any more until he heard her out. "That could change her life. And you saw how calm and good he was with her. It could change him, too."

Clint narrowed his eyes in that way he had, as if to say no one in his right mind could believe such a thing.

"She's never gone to school anyplace longer than six months and she's shy—you know that—so she has no friends. You heard her talking to that horse. It'd break her heart to tell her to stay away from him now."

"I don't want to hear it."

He turned and started walking toward the open door of the barn as if to demonstrate that fact.

Cait went with him, staying at his side as stubbornly as a sticker burr.

"I don't want to think about it," she said.

He threw her a sideways glance. An irritated glance.

"You're not training your students *too* well," he snapped. "She went into a stall with a stud horse she knew nothing about."

"She felt she knew him. From a dream. How could I know to warn them about that?"

He gave an acquiescent little shrug.

"I did tell them to be slow and calm going in, to

never let the horse turn his back on them, always to give themselves enough room.''

"Which she didn't," he said harshly. "She was up against the wall half the time."

Cait had no answer for that.

They walked out through the wide, west door into the fast-cooling air and the last of the sunset. Clint stopped to look at the sky.

She needed to get back to her class, needed to watch them all go around the arena one more time before dark, needed to talk to them about their latest lesson. And about going into stalls of strange horses and always fastening stalls and gates, just to be on the safe side.

She would. In a few minutes. But everything with Kristen was hanging in the balance here. She knew instinctively that once Clint made his final decision, that was it. There'd be no changing it.

"I couldn't believe Kristen's voice," she said quietly. "And that song. It's incredible, coming from someone so young."

He didn't say anything. He was staring off into the distance, as if trying to hold the last of the color in the sky by his sheer will.

Finally he spoke.

"She said she dreamed it."

"Yes. Kristen believes Midnight is her Nighthorse and he gives her strength. Did you notice that she even joked with you about his name, when normally she'd be way too shy to even speak to you?"

He watched the sky.

"That dream horse becoming a real horse gives her faith in her own instincts," Cait said. "It could help her take the next step to faith in God."

Clint gave her a doubtful, sideways glance.

"It's true," she said. "We all have an instinct to want to trust God."

He surprised her then.

"I wish I could," he said, "but after all the losses we've taken in the last few years, I feel I have to take care of everything myself."

"He'll help you if you ask," she said quietly. "I learned that from John."

He turned his head to look at her.

"You've had a terrible loss, too, Cait. I'm glad you have faith."

She wouldn't let him look away.

"So do you," she said. "You're just refusing to use it."

The look held.

"Have a little faith now, Clint. Maybe God brought Kristen here because of Midnight. It can't hurt to let her find out."

"It could hurt her a lot. She has no business fooling with that horse, of all the horses on this ranch."

"She doesn't have to be alone with him."

"I'm not turning that colt over to *you* and her, either. He's too unpredictable."

Cait took a long, deep breath and sent up a wordless prayer that she wasn't about to go too far.

"Clint, you have a connection with that colt, too, you know. I saw it when you rode him."

He jerked around to glare at her.

Her temper flared. Good grief! He had so much. He could give this little bit.

"She lives in a *car,* for goodness sake!"

"We'll all be living in cars if she gets hurt and sues the ranch," he said.

"You can't control *everything,*" she cried. "Get over it!"

Then, more calmly, she said, "We can do this, Clint. We can make sure she doesn't get hurt."

Finally, after an age, he said, "All right. I'll do it. But I'm already going 9-0 all day, as it is. To make up for the time I lose, you'll have to help me with some chores."

She looked into his eyes. They were gray and intense as rain clouds gathering.

"All right," she said, "it's a deal."

Then she wondered whether she could survive the storm.

Chapter Nine

Three days later everybody was predicting a tornado, because the weather had stayed warm and windy—much more like March or April than January. That evening, Clint drove toward the ranch through the late afternoon and wished with every mile that it *would* storm.

Not a tornado. No, what he needed was a great, wild, West Texas thunderstorm rolling in to fill the sky with thunder and lightning and rain to lash the land into submission. Maybe it could do the same for the turmoil inside him.

His headlights picked out a tumbleweed rolling across the road. The wind pushed his four-door dually around as if it were a toy. He sped up.

If he couldn't even bring himself to have a date anymore, if he couldn't think of anyone to ask out except the one woman he *couldn't* ask out, he was going to have to find some kind of drastic remedy.

But it wasn't just dating. If he couldn't even entertain himself, by himself, in a town as big as San Antonio—if he couldn't get interested in buying a truck or a new horse trailer with living quarters or some antique tack or a rare book about Texas history or in calling up an old buddy to go out and have a steak and a few laughs, or even in going to the zoo, for heaven's sake, he had better just stay home. Stay on the ranch and work—that was what he should do, even if he didn't like it that everybody already thought of him and the ranch as synonymous.

Clint McMahan *was* the Rocking M. That was the general assumption, and he could say that they were right. It had become so true that he didn't know what else to do with himself.

He shook his head ruefully as he turned onto the ranch road. Ever since he'd become so restless six or eight months ago, he'd intended to date a different woman every week or go into Austin or San Antonio or do *something* to get off the ranch. Well, he might as well give that up.

Stay home and ride the colts in secret and watch sports on TV. That was his life these days, and he should just get used to it. Getting off the ranch for a while didn't do him any good. No good at all.

What *would* do him good would be to forget about Cait. He should find excuses to get out of the Kristen-Midnight deal. He should hide out every day when it came time for her class. He should pretend Cait was spending all her time over at Roy Bassett's ranch as she used to do. He should pretend she wasn't around.

But as he drove toward headquarters through the quick-falling darkness, he kept glancing toward the old barn and arena where Cait gave her lessons. A couple of sets of headlights were coming down the hill. She'd said she was going to wind it up early tonight because of the weather. She'd told him that when he'd begged off helping Kristen and Midnight this evening, saying that he had errands in town.

Which he had. That was the honest truth. He wasn't going to take time away from work to drive into San Antonio *just* to try to entertain himself.

Actually, he'd gone to pick up the new custom-made cutting saddle himself instead of sending someone else *because* he needed a break from Kristen and Midnight. And Cait.

Seemed his emotions might be getting mixed up in all their business. Maybe. And he needed to keep a bit of distance.

Firmly he turned the truck to the right, to take the road to the house instead of the one to the left that led to her barn. Where she would be at this minute, checking to make sure the stalls were fastened and the aisle was clean and the equipment in the right place.

But *he* wasn't going there. He was going home to show off his new saddle, have a light dinner and then get a good night's sleep. Every person and every animal on the ranch, himself included, had been extra fractious all day because of the impending change in barometric pressure, and he was exhausted. Some real sleep would be just the ticket to ease his troubled mind.

He did drive straight to the house without looking back once to see if Cait was coming down the hill in her battered old pickup. He did show his new saddle to Bobbie Ann, Delia and LydaAnn and accept their compliments on the design and the color and the leather tooling and silver trimmings that he'd chosen. He did eat dinner with them—Bobbie Ann's delicious pot roast and silky-smooth mashed potatoes, green beans and carrots and homemade bread. But he did not get a good night's sleep.

As a matter of fact, he got no sleep at all until nearly morning.

The minute he went to his room and set his foot in the bootjack, the phone rang. Manuel. Lucky, his best cutter, was colicking. By the time he got to the barn, so was one of the customers' good pleasure horses.

"This mare always colics when the weather makes a change," Manuel said, leading both of them up and down the aisle of the barn. "But Lucky, he's not like that."

Clint took over with his own horse and they kept them both moving. The assistant trainers both came to help. Joe Gaines, the pleasure trainer, called their regular veterinarian, Ward Lincoln. He was out on an emergency call. There was no way to tell how long it might take.

Someone suggested calling Darcy.

"She needs her rest," Clint said. "And it's a rough night. I don't want to be getting her out in it."

He hoped he never would be responsible for taking that happy, peaceful look out of Jackson's eyes, not for a minute.

An hour later Lucky seemed comfortable enough to put him back into his stall.

Then he took Midnight out of his. The horse had lifted his head and smelled the wind and had run and bucked and reared and run some more in the outdoor run all afternoon, but instead of tiring him out, combined with the weather, it had fired him up. He was pacing his stall and whinnying so much he had the whole barnful worked up.

"He'll have them all so nervous they'll be colicking, too," Clint said to Manuel. "I'm turning him out in the indoor."

But the minute he led the colt out of the barn, the first thing that met his eye was more trouble. Still more trouble. All over again.

Cait's horses. There they went—the buckskin mare and the roan, racing down the road past the barn like shadows in the glow of the security lights. Clint turned and stared up the hill, but it was too dark to see the barn or whether any more of its residents were leaving it.

From that direction, though, came a loud, far-carrying whinny, somebody calling to the escaping stablemates.

Clint stopped in his tracks and jerked on the halter

to stop the dancing colt. Lightning flashed, cloud to ground and very whitely bright, showing at least one more loose horse in the door of Cait's barn. His stomach clutched as if a portentous hand had closed around it and, for a moment, he couldn't breathe.

His patience vanished.

The wind was worse than ever, but when it temporarily died a little, he heard pounding hooves up on the hill.

He'd had enough.

Clint pivoted on his heel and led Midnight right back into the barn, then handed the lead rope to Joe.

"If you will," he said tightly, "please turn him out in the indoor for me."

He looked at Manuel, then back at Joe.

"Can y'all manage without me for a while?"

"*Sí,*" Manuel said. "The mare, she's coming around, too."

"If you have an emergency, and you still haven't heard from Ward, call Jackson and ask him if Darcy's able to come out," he said. "I'll be back."

He was in his truck and on the road that led to the highway before his vision cleared. He hadn't been this angry in years, if ever.

But it wasn't all anger that was churning him up inside. He clamped his jaw. It was purpose.

His purpose was to make everybody associated with the Rocking M take responsibility for his or her own actions. To take the consequences of his or her own decisions.

He stopped at the highway, looked both ways and

then peeled out in the direction of Roy Bassett's ranch, tires squealing in the night. Cait was no exception to that rule. He'd told her from the get-go that she wasn't.

Cait sat straight up in bed at the huge clap of thunder, her heart beating like a jackhammer. She must've fallen asleep without realizing it—rain was coming in through her open window.

The loud crack of noise came again. It wasn't thunder. It was a savage pounding on the door. Her door. The *outside* door, not the one that opened into the aisle of the barn.

"Cait! It's Clint! Open up!"

Her heart rose recklessly. Clint. Clint was here.

A flaming thrill rocketed through her veins, which paralyzed her where she sat.

"*Cait!* Are you in there?"

The door burst open and there he was, inside her small room, filling it with his big body and the wind, heavy with the humidity of the coming storm. And with his anger.

She grabbed the sheet with both hands and held it to her chest in spite of the fact she was wearing a huge T-shirt that covered her to her knees. Then her quick instincts kicked in and she scrambled sideways to flip the switch on the wall beside the bed. The sudden light blinded her, made her eyes narrow to a squint.

Clint didn't so much as blink. He advanced on her without missing a beat and for one heart-stopping moment, and then another, and still another, there was more—much more—than anger in his burning look.

Then nothing but that gray storm showed in his eyes and he tore his gaze from hers to sweep the whole room with one glance.

"Where's your stuff?" he demanded. "Get what you need for tonight, and tomorrow I'll send somebody for the rest."

"I'm not getting out of this bed until you tell me what's going on! What are you *doing?*"

"Taking you out of here."

"You're not taking me anywhere. I go where I want to go."

"Get up, Cait."

He charged across to the closet, threw open the door and jerked a duffel bag from the shelf.

"You put that back! It's mine! You have no business in my closet."

"Come on," he said. "What do you need?"

"Some privacy," she snapped. "Some respect. Who do you think you *are,* Clint McMahan?"

He turned and crossed the room again, grabbing the pair of jeans she'd thrown across a chair and stuffing them into the bag while he headed for the minuscule bathroom area. All of this without so much as another glance at her.

"While I've got my back turned, get up and get some clothes on," he said. "It's raining out there."

"But not in here," she said stoutly, ignoring the fact that the windowsill was getting soaked.

"You're not staying in here."

Her famous temper overcame her shock and surprise in a heartbeat.

"Oh, yes, I am. Didn't you hear me? I'm not leaving this bed. It's the middle of the night and I need my sleep because *I* have to work."

"So do I," he growled. "And I'm not sleeping, am I?"

"I can't tell," she snapped. "You're either sleepwalking or out of your mind."

"Get your clothes on, Cait."

"I will not."

She couldn't see past him, but from the clattering noises he was making, she knew he must be sweeping her toiletries off the shelf and into the bag.

"Clint, stop it!" she yelled. "Get away from my things. You have no right…"

He didn't stop. He didn't turn around.

"Get some clothes on."

"I'm plenty decent," she said. "You get *out* of here."

He ignored that order and moved to the bureau.

"You'd better think twice," she said through clenched teeth. "Or I'll throw you out of here on your ear."

He yanked open the top drawer and dumped its contents on top of what he'd taken from the bathroom.

"You and whose army?"

He tossed the careless words over his shoulder without even turning around.

"I have weapons," she said. "I've been on my own in worse neighborhoods than this."

That didn't faze him, either.

"Do your worst," he said, "but you're coming with me."

He jerked the second drawer open.

"Look," she said sarcastically as he pulled it all the way out to empty it, too, "used underwear doesn't bring anything at garage sales and you can't pawn it."

"But *you* can wear it," he said, using that same mocking tone.

He dumped her socks and panties and bras into the bag, too, set the drawer on the floor, slid the straps of the bag onto his shoulder, strode straight to the bed and swept Cait up into his arms. All in one fluid motion that surprised her beyond belief.

"What are you *doing?*" she cried, fighting to get free.

She couldn't even get her arms loose from the sheet he'd grabbed up with her.

"Kidnapping you."

"You are *not.*"

Cait took a deep breath and arched her back, kicking against the tangle of the sheet and fighting to get her hands free, but it did no good. It didn't even slow Clint down.

He was so sure of himself that he held her in only one arm as he paused to bend over and pick up something. She tried to seize her chance, but even then, he had her in an iron grip.

Unceremoniously he slapped her boots into her lap.

"You can help," he said as he straightened and strode toward the door. "I shouldn't have to carry everything."

"Wha-a-t?" Cait cried, still struggling. "You're the one who—"

"Cait? Everything all right in here?"

It was Roy's voice.

Clint stopped. There she was, in his arms, wrapped in a sheet with her boots in her lap.

And there was Roy. In the open doorway. Where the rain was also coming in.

Roy's ruddy face flushed even more as he took in the whole scene before him.

"Sorry," he said. "I didn't mean to interrupt anything. I just came out to check the horses one more time and saw your door open and..."

Roy stopped talking, not knowing where to go after that.

"Clint," he said, with a little nod of greeting. "I didn't see your truck."

"Thanks for dropping by, Roy," Clint said smoothly. "I wanted to see you before we left. Cait's quitting this job. You can send her mail to the Rocking M."

Roy's mouth fell open about as far as Cait's did.

"What?" she cried. "No! I'm not..."

Clint ignored her, and the force of his look kept Roy's eyes on his.

"I'll be sending somebody over later this morning

to clean out her room,'' he said, and started for the door again. "We'll be seeing you, Roy."

"That's fine if it has to be," Roy said, stepping out of Clint's way, "but I sure hate to lose you, Cait. Has something happened around here that I don't know about?"

"No, Roy," she said quickly. "He's kidnapping me. I'm not quitting and I'll be back as soon as we get this straightened out. Don't hire anybody else for my job."

Clint turned sideways to get himself and Cait through the door, boots, bag and all, and stepped out into the rain. Cait gasped as the cold drops hit her face and the shoulder that wasn't tucked into the curve of Clint's big body.

"I hear Jerry Watson's assistant is looking to leave him," Clint yelled back at Roy. "You might call over there. He's a hardworking kid."

"Don't you do it, Roy," Cait screeched as the rain grew colder and heavier. "Don't you give my job away!"

She tried to look over Clint's shoulder to see whether Roy heard her or not. Clint started to run.

At his truck he opened the door and tumbled her out of his arms onto the passenger seat, then locked her door and threw the bag into the back seat as he climbed in over her and the gearshift to get to the driver's seat. Her boots fell, one onto the floor, the other over the gearshift toward the back since she didn't have her hands free.

"What are you *doing?*" she cried. "Go around!"

"And take a chance on you jumping out and running? No way am I chasing you through the rain."

Cait realized that that idea hadn't occurred to her. She hadn't seriously considered trying to get away from him since…since…

Well, since…since Roy had shown up. No, since Clint had scooped her up into his well-muscled arms and held her tight against his well-muscled chest.

Her little voice of truth scoffed at her as he twisted his big frame around to sit behind the wheel.

She had not seriously tried to get away from him since the moment he burst into her room in the middle of the night and began mishandling her belongings in the most obnoxious, rudest, most high-handed way possible.

She, who had once been known in a certain neighborhood of Chicago as Fighting Cait O'Doyle, had not seriously considered either running from Clint the intruder or using her hard-won martial-arts skills on him and throwing him out the same way he'd come in, *or* calling for help. That first thrill she'd felt when he'd yelled his name through the door was still with her.

Being shut up in this truck with him, with the heater now blasting and the powerful chug-chug of the diesel starting to carry them out to the highway was another thrill. It felt safe in here. It felt wonderful. She was with Clint.

Alone with Clint.

He smelled of horses and sweat and leather and rain and dust, too, and he just smelled like Clint.

And she ought to be ashamed of herself for letting him push her around this way.

"Clint, you ought to be ashamed of yourself."

He threw her a glance, and in the glow of the running lights she saw the corners of his mouth twitch. He shifted gears. The back of his hand brushed her knee through the sheet.

Just that slight, brief touch heated her blood. She tried to ignore that fact.

"How come?"

"People get life in federal prison for kidnapping."

"I'm not scared," he said.

"Why not?"

"Somebody has to press charges."

She bristled.

"Well! You're pretty sure of yourself, aren't you? I might surprise you and do just that."

He grinned to himself.

"In fact," she said sharply, "you are *so* sure of yourself that you left the motor running when you burglarized my home."

"Quick getaway," he said. "That much I do know about committing a crime."

His sidelong, teasing look made her heart beat even faster. He held her gaze for a long minute. Thank goodness they were still on Roy's ranch road and nobody else was out this time of night.

"It's too hot in here," she said.

Then she broke the look and started trying to get her arms out of the sheet.

"It's a diesel," he said as he turned off the heater. "Best to leave 'em running.

"And," he said, "as I've been telling you over and over again, best to get into some clothes."

That stirred her temper again.

"Forget it, Mr. Boss Man. I'm wearing my T-shirt and sheet until I get to the Rocking M. Until I know the reason you're taking me there. If I don't like it, I'm going back to bed."

She freed her hands and, with an angry huff, settled the sheet around her shoulders.

"Riding in a sheet's liable to scare your horses into running even farther."

"*What?*"

"Clothes to ride in," he said, and he sounded angry again. "Dressed or not, Caitlin, when we pull up to the barn, you're gonna ride and gather your own horses. This nonsense has got to stop. Now."

A chill ran over her. And not even because her horses were loose again.

Because she had not even *thought* about her horses. They had not entered her mind. Not once.

Which was unforgivable. Totally. She didn't deserve to *have* any horses.

Any other time—with the sudden appearance of *any* other person who was keeping her horses—her first guess would've been that there was some problem with them.

But Clint had come roaring into her room in the middle of the night, for heaven's sake, and her mind had not even gone near her horses.

Which was not only unforgivable but insane. Some terrible glitch in her mind had been created by her feelings for Clint. This was dangerous. If she didn't get those feelings under control, there could be real trouble.

She turned and got up on her knees, keeping the sheet around her waist, scrabbled in the bag on the back seat, turned everything out of it to get to the jeans in the bottom, and grabbed at a rolled-up pair of socks as they tumbled toward the floor.

"They're out *again?*" she said. "Somebody let them out on a night like this? Now, that's not a prank, it's a crime. They could get hurt. This wind's strong enough to create some flying debris, and if it turns into a tornado..."

She sat back down again and frantically started fighting to get the jeans on while modestly keeping the sheet over her. Finally she could zip them beneath the long T-shirt.

"When we find out who's doing this, I intend to ban him or her from the ranch," Clint said tightly. "If it's one of your students, get ready."

Cait fumbled for her socks, stuffed her chilly feet into them. She started trying to find both boots. It seemed impossible that it was one of her kids who was letting the horses out. She would fight that idea to her last breath, but life took strange turns.

Her heart dropped, even at the possibility. She was already getting more and more attached to those troubled teenagers. To every single one of them.

"Clint, you're overwrought," she said. "It's because you're a control freak. Don't worry, we'll get the answer to this riddle. Maybe tonight.''

He turned to scowl at her.

"Control freak? I am not."

"You are so." She frowned back. "Look at what you've done tonight. Just tonight, alone."

She dropped her boot at her feet and used both hands to tick off her points.

"You burst into my bedroom without waiting for me to open the door—trying to intimidate me, I suppose. You packed a bag I didn't want packed. You grabbed me out of my bed and carried me out of my own place while I was trying to stay there."

She matched him scowl for scowl.

"And you quit my job. You quit my job for me, Clint! The very nerve of it! If that's not being a control freak, I don't know what is!"

He dismissed all that with a wave of his hand.

"And don't try to tell me that that's how anybody—any normal person—would behave."

He flicked her a glance at the word *normal*, but he'd already gone past caring what she thought.

"Maybe we'll find out tonight, as you say," he said, barely slowing down and looking both ways before he turned the wheel to take them out onto the highway, "or maybe not until tomorrow or next week. But however long it takes, you'll be right there to take care of your own animals, Cait. From now on. As long as your school lasts."

"No way," she cried, thrusting one foot into her boot. "I've got a job and I'm going back to it! Roy will hopefully put this down to a quarrel of some kind between you and me. He won't hold it against me."

Her temper rose at the thought of not getting to show the horse Overtime after all the hard work she'd put in on him.

"I knew that you just can't stand it unless you control everything," she said tightly, "but I would never have guessed that you'd take it upon yourself to tell Roy to go hire somebody else. That's way out of line, Clint."

"Get over it," he said bluntly. "You've got a job on the Rocking M."

Then, to her surprise, he lost his anger and gave her a look that held nothing but seriousness.

"Think about it, Cait. Which is more important? Showing those horses of Roy's or doing all you can for those kids? For Kristen? And Joey? And Warren and Darren who don't rhyme? You're changing their lives here, Cait."

It caught her so off guard she got a huge lump in her throat.

Finally she was able to say, "So are you. Especially for Kristen."

They rode in silence the rest of the way to the ranch, with Cait praying her heart out.

Lord, is Clint right? Do You want me to put the school first and live on the Rocking M? Even though being near him makes me so crazy I forget about my horses?

"I'll make sure you're horseback," Clint said

huskily as they rolled under the arching sign that proclaimed the Rocking M. "I'll put you aboard any show horse you want. Just name it."

Shocked, she stared at him while the wind tore at the truck and the lightning flashed.

When she could talk again, she didn't know what to say except, "Thanks, Clint."

"No problem," he said.

When they pulled up to the barn, Manuel came out and Clint rolled his window down.

"Go to bed, boss," Manuel called. "We put 'em all up, and I've got Diego sleeping in that barn."

"Thanks, Manuel. Good man."

They rode on to the main house in silence again. While they did, Cait turned and picked up her scattered possessions to put them back into the bag. She wished she could do the same with her thoughts and feelings.

She felt as if a tornado had formed right over her head, that it had dipped down and picked up her whole life and turned it into a whirlwind of flying debris. It had done the same to her own self, too, or she wouldn't be here right now, arriving at the Rocking M in the middle of the night, alone with Clint.

Clint's offer to buy her a show horse was enough to blow her completely away.

And the fact that she hadn't told him the truth—which was that she would never, in her wildest dreams and on her most desperate day, consider letting him make such a gesture toward her—was even more shocking than that.

Chapter Ten

Cait got out as soon as Clint stopped the truck, slammed the door behind her and, clutching her overflowing bag in both hands, ran through the rain toward the house. He was beside her, though, by the time she reached the steps to the porch.

He took her bag from her.

She reached to take it back, saying, "I can carry it."

He didn't let her have it.

"Be nice," he said, teasing her. "Be a lady and just say thank you."

He put his hand under her elbow as they dashed up the shallow steps, his big body blocking hers from the force of the wind.

"*You* certainly haven't acted like a *gentleman* tonight."

His touch, that magical touch, and his teasing put

a smile in her voice that she hadn't intended. She was trying to make a serious point here.

Wasn't she?

"*What?* Look at me right now," he said, and took off his hat and put it on her head. "Now what do you say? I'm protecting you from the rain while I'm getting soaked."

Cait laughed.

"For two seconds," she said as they stepped up onto the porch. "Now we're under the roof—"

A voice from the darkness interrupted.

"Clint? Caity?"

Cait and Clint huddled together, frozen for an instant, like children caught with their hands in the cookie jar.

Bobbie Ann stepped out of the dark into the glow from the yard light that showed the way to the door. She and Clint were already standing in it.

With Clint's hand on her elbow and his hat on her head.

Lord, I don't care about Roy's opinion, but please don't let Bobbie Ann think there's something between me and Clint. That I'm forgetting John...

Clint recovered use of his tongue.

"Ma, what're you doing out here in the dark?"

"Checking on the porch furniture," she said slowly. "Turning the rocking chairs up against the wall so they'll be out of the wind and rain. I couldn't sleep and I looked out...and...the rain was getting heavier...."

Clearly she wasn't thinking about what she was saying. She was thinking about what she was seeing.

Her blue eyes, wide with surprise, were the very same startling blue color as Jackson's. They fixed on Clint's face and then on Cait's. Each only for a second. Then she smiled.

"Welcome, Cait," she said. "What a nice surprise. You're stayin' the night?"

"I...I hope it won't be any trouble," Cait said. "Clint...insisted that I come over here and take care of my own horses."

Bobbie Ann raised her eyebrows and considered that.

"Well, son," she said, "I hope you were a gentleman about it."

They all laughed.

"I was, Ma," Clint said as he guided Cait across the porch. "I'm always a gentleman, no matter what you might hear to the contrary."

"I'm glad, son," Bobbie Ann said wryly. "It's a comfort to me to know it."

He let go of Cait to hold the door for her and his mother.

"You ladies go ahead."

He waited a beat.

"See what I mean, Ma?"

"That'll do, Clint, honey," Bobbie Ann drawled. "Actually, I never had a serious doubt."

They laughed again as she put an arm around Cait. When they were all inside, Clint closed the door and shut out the noise of the storm.

"I'm so glad you're here, Cait," Bobbie Ann said. "Let's put you in the room you used for Christmas. I'll take you up there and get you settled..."

Clint interrupted.

"I'll do that so you can get on back to bed, Ma," he said. "You know the room's perfect, anyhow, and if it isn't, Cait knows where the towels are."

Cait caught a trace of a smile on Bobbie Ann's face again.

"Very well," she said as she gave Cait a little hug. "See y'all in the morning."

"Good night," they chorused, and headed for the stairs while Bobbie Ann turned toward the hall that led to the master suite.

"I notice you're not quite so sure of yourself now," Cait said. "You didn't tell her I'd be here more than one night."

"Because she'd have rushed up here and started painting your room and making a new bedspread," he said. "You wouldn't have gotten a minute's sleep."

She gave him a teasing glance.

"So you were only thinking of me?"

"Right. I'm an unselfish kind of guy."

"Oh, *right*," she said sarcastically. "Why didn't I realize that?"

But as they climbed the stairs side by side and the wonderful old house folded its arms around her again, she had to say something. This was scary beyond belief, the way she loved the security and the solidity of this ranch.

Scary that she felt she belonged on the Rocking M.

Because, in the long, long run she couldn't stay. She was a member of the family, yes, but feeling the way she did about Clint, she couldn't stay.

She had to reach for the reins of her own life, since he'd snatched them away.

Outside the door of her room, the room that felt more like hers now than the tiny house she'd shared so briefly with John, she stopped and turned to take the bag. Clint ignored the gesture, walked into the room and dropped it onto the bed.

He filled up her room just as he was filling up her thoughts and threatening to fill up her life if she stayed.

"Listen, Clint. In the morning I'm calling Roy to tell him to hold my job open until I can get this all straightened out."

He stood there for a long moment with his hand on the bedpost. For once, the storm was gone from his eyes.

"It's a done deal, Cait. You just don't know it yet."

Without warning, he reached out and brushed a hand across her thick curls. Gently, very gently. Raindrops flew everywhere.

She barely felt them, because her shoulders were already damp from running through the rain.

For a long, long moment she thought he was going to kiss her. Cait's heart racketed in her chest.

"Better get out of those wet clothes," he said finally.

Then he walked past her, across the room and out into the hall.

"Good night," he called.

"Good night."

He closed her door behind him.

Cait ripped off her wet shirt, kicked off her boots, got out of her jeans and threw herself across the bed, facedown. Without lifting her head, she reached with one hand to pull the comforter over her.

Now that she was alone, she could think. She could figure this out.

Clint was right in saying that what happened to her kids was more important than her job. In God's eyes, that had to be true.

But she had to earn money or there'd be no horsemanship school. And if she was to be a trainer someday and have her own business, she had to keep building her reputation now. She had to keep showing Roy's horses.

What should she do?

The house creaked and settled as it sheltered her. The wind howled around its corners and rain pelted the windowpanes, but now the storm sounded very far away.

Before Cait had another thought, sleep took her.

* * *

The next morning, Clint slept in. To his complete consternation, he woke to bright sunlight and an unfamiliar, well-rested feeling.

Cait was right next door.

That was his first conscious thought.

It froze him in place. He'd have to be careful now. He'd have to try not to be around her too much or touch her at all.

Because his body remembered how she'd felt when he'd carried her to the truck: her weight in his arms, her skin against his—just a bit of it, here and there, like silk in the places not covered by the cotton sheet. She was tall enough that her face had been so near his. Near enough to kiss.

Her hair had brushed his face with the fragrance of lemons and roses and rain, all mixed with the warm smell of Cait just wakened from sleep. He had been a strong man not to kiss her then.

Forget that. He'd been out of his mind not to kiss her.

No, he had been out of his mind to take her in his arms in the first place.

He had been out of his mind. Absolutely, totally, out of his mind last night.

Sighing, he rolled out of bed and slapped his feet to the floor. What he'd done was stupid, as far as his personal feelings were concerned. And as far as gossip was concerned, too. Now Roy Bassett probably thought there was something going on between him and Cait and half the people he knew would hear about it before sundown.

In those respects, it was the wrong thing to do—

he would admit that in a heartbeat. But for the ranch, it was the right thing to do. By far.

If Cait was going to have that school here, then she had to *stay* here and supervise the horses, as well as the teenagers. He and his hands had taken enough time from their regular chores to chase her horses around.

Yes, he had brought Cait here for the good of the ranch.

It had been the right thing to do. Somehow, he knew that in his gut, which was rapidly convincing his head.

Quickly he showered and dressed. Then, with his hand on his doorknob, he stood very still and listened. The walls of the old house were thick. So were the doors. Cait might be close by or she might not. He'd just have to take his chances.

Cait stared in consternation at the storm damage to her arena. One whole section of the fence, the east end of it, had been blown down. The planks, so old they were weathered to a silvery gray, lay flat on the ground and the posts were scattered haphazardly on top of them. Surely it had been a tornado that she and Clint had been out in last night. The wind had jerked the posts, concrete and all, right out of the holes they'd been set in for years.

Great. Here she was, devoting her whole life to her school now, according to Clint's decree, and she had no place to hold class. If she'd had her cell phone with her, she'd have called Roy to save her job and then asked him for the use of his arena for her classes.

But her cell phone, like her wallet and her keys and her truck, was still at Roy's. Until whoever went over there on Clint's orders brought them to her.

She should've thrown a fit last night and sent Clint on his way before he physically carried her out of her room.

So why hadn't she?

She didn't want to think about that.

Standing on the side of the low hill, she turned and looked at the layout below. It made no sense whatsoever to haul these horses all over creation when there were other arenas right here.

Lord, is it really true? Do I belong here? This morning I feel even more strongly that I'm supposed to be on the Rocking M.

Resolutely she turned, stepped over and through the shattered fence and went on into the barn. While she rode, she'd think some more about calling Roy and she'd think some more about staying here and God would lead her to know what was right for her.

She smiled as she went to get her saddle and pad. There'd been an old man who was a groom at the track when she first learned to ride who used to say that God could speak best to a person who was horseback because then they were closer to Him.

Today she would be horseback. She'd take care of her own horses and she'd ride each one as much as it wanted to be ridden. She'd have as much solitude as she needed.

But she hadn't even finished saddling the first one, the short roan gelding, when she heard the powerful engine of a truck coming up the hill. One glance out the wide double door told her it was Clint.

Well, at least he wasn't horseback. She could ride off across the pasture and leave him behind if he bossed her too much.

Or made her want to be near him.

He parked, got out of the truck and came in as she went back to the tack room for a bridle.

"Don't you trust me?" she asked mildly as she grabbed one and stepped back out into the aisle.

No way was she going to let him come into that tiny room with her again and make her want him to kiss her.

"What d'you mean?"

"You told me to take care of my own horses, and here you are checking up on them yourself."

He grimaced and shook his head as if she were a hopeless case and just kept walking down the aisle of the barn to the east door. Then he stopped and looked out at the wreckage of the fence.

"Hold your class in the indoor until we get this fixed," he said.

Miracle of miracles.

"I'm not sure I heard you correctly," she said, half teasing and half not.

She buckled the bridle, picked up the reins and led the stocky roan horse toward him.

"Did you say the indoor, Clint?"

He turned and leaned back against the edge of the doorway as he watched her walk toward him.

"You heard me."

She walked on past him and held the horse outside in the warm sun.

"I'll accept your invitation," she said. "Thank you."

"Not a problem."

He looked past her, stared thoughtfully out across the ranch, much as she had done a few minutes earlier. His profile was so powerful she couldn't look away.

"You remind me of a hero in an old Western movie," she said, "looking out over the valley to see if the bad guys are here yet."

He turned and looked at her, with a quick, serious look at first, and then with a glint of mischief in his eyes.

"I'm glad you said 'old Western movie' instead of 'old hero,'" he said.

She grinned.

"Maybe I got that backward."

"I just *look* old because you and your kids are making me turn gray," he drawled.

"But now that's over," she said. "I'm here now to take care of my own business. You won't ever have to give me or my horses or my kids another minute's thought."

"Is that a promise?" he said, lightly sarcastic.

She thought he was going to say something more, but then he turned and gazed off into the distance again, frowning a little as if he were trying to work out some problem or make a decision about something.

What was going on with him, anyhow? First he offered to buy her a show horse and now he was sharing his precious indoor arena.

Yet he behaved as if he had something to tell her that he couldn't quite bring himself to say.

That offer to put her on a world-class show horse, for example—that had been nothing short of bizarre, considering the attitude he'd always held toward her. It had sounded almost as if he'd been trying to bribe her to go along with his decision that she should move to the Rocking M. Maybe he'd been angry and he'd wanted to make her take care of her own horses, and he'd decided he'd get his way no matter what it took to do it.

And maybe he was sorry now, maybe he thought it was a mistake for her to live here. Had he come over here to tell her that?

She had to know. Suddenly she *needed* to hear his feelings put into words, because she couldn't read his actions at all.

"What're you thinking?" she asked softly. "Are you wishing you'd left me at Roy's?"

Her stomach clutched. Suddenly she didn't want to go back to Roy's. She wanted to spend every day right here, riding over the rolling hills of the Rocking M in the winter sunlight, thinking of what to do next with her students. When summer came, she might hold two sessions a day.

But Clint didn't say anything. Her stomach tightened into a knot. It was like waiting for the other shoe to fall.

She persisted.

"Have you talked to Roy today?"

Obviously startled, he looked at her and shook his head.

"What would I say to Roy? I told him everything he needed to know last night."

"You still hold to that?" she said.

He held her gaze with his for a heartbeat. Then another.

"Yep."

His look was so intense it took away her breath. He shouldn't look at her this way.

"You know you shouldn't have carried me out of there like that, don't you?" she said. "Now Roy will be telling everyone he talks to that there's something going on between us."

Clint raised one eyebrow.

"Is it true?"

"Well, no," she said quickly.

Too quickly.

His gray eyes narrowed, then searched her face.

Did he wish, as she did, that something *was* going on between them? Being this close to him made her feel reckless and bold, made her want that as much as she'd ever wanted anything in her life.

She'd loved John so much, but she'd never felt exactly like *this* before.

Right now, this minute, she had to walk away

from him. She had to step up on her horse and *ride* away at a good, quick pace.

She turned toward the saddled roan, and when she did, a movement in the barn caught her eye. Daisy's head was hanging over the stall door and she appeared to be nosing at its latch.

Cait watched her. She did it again.

"Clint," she whispered. "Come here."

Instantly he was at her side.

Daisy's head disappeared back into the stall and then, slowly, the door began to swing open.

Clint grasped Cait's arm and pulled her with him as he stepped back outside the door to hide from Daisy. As they peered around the corner into the barn, the warm shape of his hand burned itself into her skin, even through the sleeve of her jean jacket. She never wanted to move again.

Daisy walked out into the aisle, threw up her head and looked around for a moment. Some of the other horses nickered at her, low in their throats. She deliberated for a minute or two, then went to the sorrel gelding's stall and started working on his latch.

"I can't believe this," Cait said, barely breathing the words.

"Wait a minute," Clint muttered.

But they both knew that this was the solution to the mystery. Daisy was the one who'd been releasing the horses from their stalls.

Sure enough, a few more nudges and she turned the gelding's latch bar with the hook up, then gradually nosed it through the loop. She even opened his door for him.

"Full service," Clint whispered.

Cait turned her head and their eyes met in such excited understanding they didn't need any words. Smiling from ear to ear, Clint squeezed her arm as if this moment were some kind of great victory for them both. Which it was.

When they looked again, the two horses had started wandering up and down the aisleway.

Clint pulled Cait even closer and put his mouth against her ear. A shivery thrill ran through her at the feel of his warm breath on her skin.

"I'll go around to the other door," he murmured. "You block this one. Let's not spend the day chasing them all over the ranch."

Then he left her.

Suddenly she felt so bereft that she couldn't even move. It didn't feel right for Clint to be gone from her side.

Finally she eased out into the middle of the wide doorway and stood quietly, still holding the reins of the roan.

Daisy chose the bay mare's stall and began fiddling with that latch. The sorrel gelding nudged her in the side, as if to hurry her along, turning her head as Clint appeared at the opposite end of the aisle.

Cait looped the reins of the roan around the outside hitching rack and walked slowly into the barn. Neither horse was very serious about escaping, so she and Clint easily drove the two of them, first the gelding, and then Daisy, back into their stalls.

"Get me some chain and a lock," Cait said, laughing. "I'm padlocking this mare in here for the rest of her natural life."

Clint laughed, too.

"No, no," he said. "Take her on the road. Daisy the Wonder Horse. Y'all can entertain at rodeos and horse shows by escaping from trailers, stalls, barns and chutes. You'll be rich and famous."

Cait flashed him a flirtatious look.

"You wouldn't be trying to get rid of us, would you?"

"Nope," he said as he looped a lead rope through the bars on the door and the side of Daisy's stall and began to tie a knot she couldn't untie. "Don't know what we'd do around here without you and Miss Daisy to entertain us."

She wished he entertained *her*. Instead of making her knees weak with his smile and her breath stop with his touch.

Cait was helping her kids rinse their sweaty mounts at the outdoor wash rack when Clint came out of the indoor arena and started down the slope toward them. They were doing the last two horses, with the rest of them attached to the nearby horse walkers to dry in the sun.

"Everybody's been asking where you were," Natalie called to him. "You've missed the whole class."

"Yeah, and now you'll have to make it up," Joey chimed in.

Clint looked startled, then pleased. He tried to hide it, though.

Cait smiled to herself. He would never admit it, and she would never have believed it a couple of weeks ago, but these kids were starting to get under his skin.

"I thought it was warm enough to rinse them off outside," she said as he walked up to them. "It feels good to be out in the sun."

"Yeah," Darren said. "We're back-to-nature cowboys."

Clint raised his eyebrows.

"So does this mean the indoor arena was too confining? You don't want to use it anymore?"

The protests rose in a chorus.

"No!"

"No, man, that place is cool!"

"We like the lounge. Can we have a party in there on our last day?"

A sudden silence fell as they all absorbed Warren's question, and six tense faces turned toward Cait.

Kristen half whispered the words everyone was thinking.

"That won't be soon, will it?"

"I'm planning for this class to go on all the way through next summer, at least," Cait said. "I hope it'll last that long."

"What about it, Clint?" Joey asked boldly. "You think so, too? End of the summer?"

Open eagerness glowed in Joey's face, which usually he kept as impassive as possible. Cait saw that Clint noticed it, too.

"Yep. Can't get out of here until you trail ride a hundred miles and learn to cut cattle."

"A-all ri-ight!"

The noise started up again as a celebration and Joey finished rinsing his horse with a flamboyant twirling of water through the air in a huge circle. The girls screamed when a few drops fell on them, and everybody laughed and started milling around.

Daisy added to the festivities by sticking her head up and trying to get a drink when the hose swept past her a second time, and Darren, who had hold of the hose in the other outdoor wash bay, squirted Joey. Joey squirted him back and the fight was on.

To their great credit, though, they both took care of their horses first—Darren handed his lead rope to Warren, and Joey threw Daisy's to a startled Kristen—before they threw themselves into their fun. Seconds later they were squirting everybody in sight and Joey turned his hose, full force, onto Clint.

For an instant everybody froze, but to their surprise, Cait's most of all, Clint just ripped off his hat, dropped it onto Cait's head and ran into the middle of the fray to wrest Darren's hose from him and turn it on Joey. Squealing and laughing, Joey ran. Clint chased him as far as the hose would reach, which was quite a way, and soaked him. Warren ran to try to get hold of Joey's hose, but Natalie already had it in her hands, and it all went on and on.

Cait got out of the way and let them play, protecting Clint's hat as best she could. They all were in it now, even Kristen, because Clint had turned the hose on her, not much, but enough to bring her into the game. The other kids must've thought she was too shy to play. He kept the game going as much as they did, all of them running and sliding on the asphalt road.

Lord, please don't let any of them get hurt.

Then she realized what she'd said.

Lord, please don't let me turn into a worrywart like Clint.

That made her laugh to herself. He'd laugh, too, when she told him his attitude was rubbing off on her.

Finally they began to wind down, and Clint, his soaked shirt clinging to his muscular back, came to shut the water off. He glanced at Kristen, who wasn't nearly as wet as the others.

"Run up to the tack room there in the indoor, will you, Kristen?" he said. "In that closet there're some jackets people have left lying around. Would you grab some of them for us?"

Cait stepped forward and signaled for attention.

"Let's not track up the tack room, since we've just swept it," she said. "When Kristen gets back, if you want to take off your wet shirt and put on something dry, go into the bathroom or the apartment in the main barn, okay?"

"Then we'll take our own horses up to our barn and *tie* them in," Natalie said.

Cait had told them the solution to the loose-horses mystery first thing when they arrived.

"*Duh,*" Joey called to her. "Only Daisy needs it. She's the only one can get out."

Kristen came back wearing a jacket and carrying some others. Some kids changed and some didn't, but they all put up their horses and started for home much faster than they normally did. They left while Clint was putting a special, quick-release fastener on Daisy's stall.

"I hope none of them catches cold," Cait said from the doorway as she waved goodbye to the last one. "The breeze is a little bit cool, but they had *so* much fun."

She turned to look at him.

"Did you?"

He grinned.

"I did."

He gathered up his tools.

"This is quick-release for humans only," he told Daisy, who was watching him suspiciously, "so in an emergency, we can get you out in a hurry. No emergency, you stay put. Hear me?"

He sauntered over to the toolbox he'd left on the battered bench that sat outside the door of the tack room. For one breathtaking moment Cait thought he was coming to her.

She wanted him to.

She wanted to feel the heavy muscles in his

arms—they showed so clearly through the wet fabric plastered to his skin. He'd rolled up the sleeves to just below the elbow; it was blue chambray, an old work shirt worn thin and soft through the years.

Years she hadn't been here. Years she hadn't known him.

She needed to get him out of this barn before she walked straight to him, laid her sweaty palms on his bare arms and stood on her toes to kiss him squarely on his mouth. Just imagining it almost made her feet move. Just thinking about it made her feel compelled to do it.

This was definitely dangerous, the two of them alone on a warm, sunny winter afternoon. All alone in a barn smelling of sweet feed and hay and horses. He should go now.

"You'd better go put some dry clothes on, yourself," Cait blurted.

He closed the box, straightened and turned to face her.

"I can't," he said, smiling as he crossed the space between them. "I'm afraid you have an ulterior motive."

For the space of one wild heartbeat, she thought he'd read her mind. He was close now. So close she couldn't move.

"What...ulterior motive?"

Her voice came out so soft and breathless she could hardly hear herself.

He shrugged carelessly, but his eyes held hers.

"You excuse me from your chores, you think I'll

excuse you from loping my cutters tomorrow while I help Kristen with Midnight.''

She tilted her head and flashed him a deliberately flirtatious look.

''Why, whatever gave you that idea? I do what I say I'll do.''

He just looked at her for the longest time, smiling a little, as if he simply liked to. As if he couldn't think of anything he'd rather do than look at her.

Then he reached out and caressed her arm, just once. It sent a heated thrill dancing through her.

''Well, then,'' he said in his deepest Texas drawl, ''I'm thinking your eyes just now promised me a kiss.''

She walked into his arms and lifted her mouth to his. It became her world before she took another breath. Hot and sweet, it drew her in and captured her.

Strong and sure, his arms surrounded her and made her feel safe forever. She surrendered. Slowly, deliberately, she put her arms around his neck and held him even closer.

He held her tighter and his kiss carried her away in a torrent of promise that seemed to have no end.

She didn't want it ever to end. Never. She kissed him back with all her heart, which put her in danger of falling if he hadn't been holding her up.

Forever. She wanted to stay in his arms forever.

At last that thought stabbed her mind into functioning.

Clint wasn't thinking about forever. Clint still blamed her about John.

She broke the kiss and pulled back, and he loosened his arms from around her. But then she looked up into his heavy-lidded gray eyes and they kissed again, quick and hard, hands gripping each other's arms, without knowing which of them started it.

But they both knew she stopped it.

John had loved her with an open heart, and nothing in the past was of any matter to him. Clint could never love her that way.

"I—I can't," she stammered, and pushed out of his embrace. "You're not...John...."

He gave her such a terrible look it withered her heart.

Then he was gone.

Chapter Eleven

Twenty-four hours had passed, and Clint was still furious. He was still so sick with the feelings Cait had inflamed in him that he hadn't eaten all day and had slept no more than three hours.

If it hadn't been for the fact that horses existed and that he could ride from before dawn until right now, five minutes before he was to meet Cait and Kristen, he didn't know what he would've done.

But it wouldn't have been pretty.

This was the tenth mount he'd been on today and he was coming back from his tenth different trail ride destination. He ought to be ready to see her.

He *was* ready to see her. He didn't *want* that, he wanted nothing so much as to stay away from her for the rest of his natural life, but he wasn't going to be the one to go back on his word and he wasn't going to run from a few bad feelings. Nope, this deal with Kristen and Midnight and Cait helping him with his chores was going to go on exactly as planned.

Never again would he allow a shred of connection between himself and Cait—except for this school business, of course—and he would not waste a ripple of emotion on her. Not one. And not a thought, either. Not a glimmer of one.

He set his jaw and rode onto the graveled lane that stretched the mile or so from the barn that, back in Old Clint's day, had been the mare motel to the present-day headquarters. Too bad that hadn't been Grandpa Clint's spirit hanging around the ranch letting the horses out, because it'd sure be a comfort to talk to the old man about now.

Back when *he* was thirty-five, life on the Rocking M must've been a whole lot more straightforward, a whole lot more...well, *set*. Grandpa hadn't been dealing with any of this nonsense about horsemanship schools for wayward teenagers and beautiful sisters-in-law kissing a man half-senseless.

Clint looked down the long, straight way to the indoor arena that appeared to be a toy building in the distance. When he'd left the house at dawn, he had put a note under Cait's door telling her to bring Kristen to meet him there. It'd be a much larger space, where they could stay farther apart. He didn't intend to be caught in tight quarters, like a stall, with her. He didn't want to be that close to her. And he didn't intend to be alone with her, ever again.

He glanced at the sun, then confirmed his guess by his watch. No doubt he'd be later than the time they had set with Kristen, but he didn't care. It'd do Cait good to have to wait for him. In fact, it'd give him a great deal of satisfaction to keep Cait waiting.

He wouldn't be the first one of them not to keep his word.

Hadn't she kissed him as if she meant it—*twice*— and then told him he wasn't John?

The hard kernel of bitterness in the middle of his gut grew in rhythm with the trotting of his mount. How could she say such a thing at a time like that?

He had had no business kissing her in the first place. What had possessed him, anyway?

He'd thought he and Cait had a friendship going on between them, plus a real attraction to each other. Something the talking heads on television would call a relationship. *That* was why he'd kissed her.

And because, truth to tell, he'd wanted to kiss her ever since he'd seen her propped up there on the fence in the indoor looking him over with those big black eyes of hers early on Christmas Eve morning. She'd been giving him one hundred percent of her attention, watching him ride.

Watching him and Midnight look like *poetry.*

Also, he had kissed her because she'd been laughing and joking with him and solving mysteries with him and depending on him to apply a lock that would keep Daisy in her stall. And she'd been sharing the kids in her school with him.

But mainly it was because she had *wanted* him to kiss her. He had seen it in her eyes. He had not imagined that look.

He relived those few moments for the thousandth time.

Truth was she had kissed him back with all her heart. She had kissed him back with a passion. She had clung to him.

Then, boom, with no warning, two heartbeats later it was all about John. His dear, quiet and faithful brother who had never been a match for such a woman as Cait.

She must have loved John, after all.

Cait spent the whole day off the ranch. She watched the time so she wouldn't be late to meet Kristen and Clint, but she would have been looking at her watch anyway. The minutes crawled by like hours. The hours felt like days. But she stayed gone, anyway.

She was the worst shopper in the entire world. She had no desire to look at bunches of beautiful, expensive, mostly useless things, much less to buy them—assuming she'd had the money—but after she went by Roy's and explained the situation to him, she spent the whole day alone in Fredericksburg, keeping to herself while sharing the sidewalks with tourists and snowbirds, prowling the furniture, clothing, knickknack, bed and bath, book, leather and Western shops as if her life depended on finding exactly the right item in each one. Getting away from the ranch, driving nearly two hours alone each way and seeing all these different people and objects, just being in a town, ought to give her a different perspective.

A different perspective ought to help her know what to do.

But she left the charming old town and started driving back to the Rocking M still trapped in the middle of the same dilemma that had brought her there. She loved Clint. In spite of trying not to.

In spite of knowing that Clint didn't love her.

That look he'd given her had proved that. It wasn't just shock that she'd brought up John's name at that moment. His eyes had been full of scorn for her.

Still, she wasn't sorry that she'd said it. She couldn't kiss Clint like that without rushing faster and harder down that slippery slope of loving him, and if she was going to love him, they had to talk about John.

No, if *they* were going to love *each other,* they had to talk about John. And that wasn't going to happen, so it was not a problem, after all, now was it?

Because if Clint loved her, he'd realize that she'd grown up poor and rough, she'd had to learn to be assertive and tough and to say what she meant and to ask for what she wanted and needed. But since Clint wasn't accustomed to that in a woman, he'd not taken that into account.

If he loved her, he'd have listened to her. He would've let her finish the sentence and he would've heard what she'd intended to say. If he loved her, he would love her for her whole self and who she was, the way John had loved her.

John had treated her better than any man she'd ever known. John had taught her about love. She would never, ever forget him.

But oh. Never had she felt this way about John.

Cait took a deep breath, punched the ''off'' button on the radio and tried to think. She loved Clint. She knew it. But maybe what she loved about him was the solid, secure, settled aspect of his life. Maybe what she really loved was the ranch.

Because, try as she would, she didn't feel at home anywhere else. In fact, she never had really, in her whole life, felt at home anywhere until John had brought her to the Rocking M.

She pressed harder on the accelerator of her battered truck. She dreaded seeing Clint today, but she'd done plenty of things in her life that she'd dreaded and she could do this one, too.

Maybe it would do her good to see that scornful look in his eyes again. Maybe, eventually, if she saw it often enough, it would kill this love she felt for him.

In the meantime, what she must remember was that nothing could come of that love, ever, because John would always stand between them. Clint would always believe that John would not have died if Cait had gone with him on that mission trip to Mexico. Clint thought if she had been there John would never have ventured onto that lonely road where a bandit shot him.

She couldn't live with that. And he couldn't, either.

A cold wind rose and blew in through her open window to whip her hair against her cheek. She turned her face to it as she drove the narrow, deserted back roads that would take her to the ranch.

That was exactly what she needed. A slap in the face to wake her up and stop her mind from running around and around the same track. She'd had one good man who loved her in her life, and that was more than many women ever had. She should be grateful for that instead of being greedy for more.

And she should get a grip on all her feelings. Home or not, she couldn't stay on the ranch if her heart was going to leap every time she saw Clint and sink to the ground every time he walked away. If he was going to scorn her for simply being who she was.

Lord, please take this feeling away from my heart. Please let me quit loving Clint.

Then, in all honesty, she added a postscript.

So I can stay on the ranch.

God had given her the idea for her horsemanship school. God had led her to start it on the Rocking M. She believed that with all her heart.

But His purpose might have been for her to learn something by being there. Maybe He'd meant for John's old home to be a temporary location for his memorial.

All right, Lord, I'll accept whatever You have planned. And I'll try to quit thinking about me. I'll try to quit thinking about Clint. Please help me do that. Please help me think about my students and listen to You. Where should I be with these kids and what should I do?

Kristen watched Cait run along the road between the indoor and outdoor arenas, two halters swinging from her shoulder. She'd said she was going to catch the cutters that Clint wanted her to lope for him and bring them back here to the indoor.

That should take a few minutes. Long enough.

She watched just a moment more, to be sure Cait wasn't going to turn back for any reason. She had promised Cait that she wouldn't go alone to get Midnight out of his stall. She had promised to wait right here for Clint.

All of which was perfect for her plan.

As soon as she was satisfied that Cait was far enough away, Kristen left the side door and headed for the tack room, walking on the balls of her feet, listening carefully to hear if anyone else came into the building. It was fairly certain that she'd be alone in here for a few minutes, and that was all she needed.

At the door she stopped, took a deep breath, squeezed her eyes shut and said her mantra for luck.

"Midnight Horse, Mountain Horse, Night Horse, Sky Horse, Black Horse bring me luck," she whispered.

Since she'd found her dream horse here, in the

flesh, she'd added the "Midnight Horse" name. Might as well—that's what Clint called him.

After that, she ran lightly across the tiled floor past the wall covered with rows and rows of bridles to the wall covered with rows and rows of saddle racks that went even higher. The saddle she was looking for had been on the end by the door to the entryway, second row up, when she'd first seen it yesterday during the water fight.

Her heart sank as she unzipped the saddle cover on the saddle on that rack. This wasn't it. This was some saddle with a flower pattern on its silver trim.

But this was the right rack, she *knew* it!

Hastily she rezipped the cover and unzipped the one below it. No. Not the right one.

She stopped and made herself take time to look down the line at the saddles that wore no covers. Yesterday the beautiful saddle had been bare—otherwise, she would never have noticed it. But today all the uncovered ones were worn and battered work saddles.

Cold disappointment made her hands shake. This might be her only chance!

She started walking down the line, looking swiftly but carefully to see if it sat underneath one of the other ones, just to make sure. Why couldn't it still be here? It had been only a day!

Kristen reached the end of the row, her heart pounding like crazy. If it was still here, it was covered.

She went back to the rack where it had been the

day before and started on the saddles near it, opening covers quickly—unzipping, lifting the cover enough to see the silver trim, zipping back again. With the fourth one, she found it!

As fast as she could, she ran to each door, then to the windows facing the end of the main barn to look out, but no one was in sight. It was late afternoon and the trainers were finished with the arena. Manuel's crew was still working way down at the stud barn.

It was meant to be! She hadn't dreamed it, but still, it was meant to be. It was meant for her to have the silver concho, or she would never have noticed that it was loose, would she?

Holding her breath, she raced back to the saddle and unzipped that whole side of its cover, pushed it open until she could get to the concho on the right side in the back. It hadn't been fixed yet.

She began to twist it, desperately, but it was on crooked. It was loose, it wasn't screwed down tight, but it was stuck at a crazy angle.

Her knees trembled. She would never get another chance like this.

Quickly she threw a sharp glance in every direction and reached into the front pocket of her jeans for the small penknife she always carried, pulled it out and opened it. Placing the short blade under the concho, she began to put a quick, rocking pressure on it, pulling at the same time with her other hand.

After what seemed an incredibly long time, despair flooded through her. It wasn't going to come off.

She gritted her teeth and pushed and pulled some more. It *had* to come off. She was going to *make* it come off. She'd never wanted anything as much as she wanted this.

Finally, suddenly, with a pull so hard that she lurched and nearly fell backward, the silver disk came free into her hand. She grabbed the saddle's horn to steady her as she dragged air into her lungs. She was dizzy. All this time, she must've been holding her breath.

She kissed the concho, polished it against her thigh, then slipped it into the pocket of the jean jacket she wore, placing it carefully beneath a small packet of tissues. She folded the knife, put it away and closed up the saddle cover.

A great, joyful melody began singing through her veins. Now, no matter when she had to leave the Rocking M, she had a souvenir with that flowing brand embossed on it. She had something of this place where her Nighthorse lived, something to keep forever.

When Clint led Midnight into the entrance to the indoor, Kristen and Cait were in the saddling bay with the horses Cait was going to ride for him. They were just finishing saddling them.

"Hey, Clint," Kristen called. "Is the Midnight Horse in a good mood today?"

"Not so you'd notice it," he said.

Cait turned to see him walking past the open doorway. Their eyes met.

"Remember I said not to ride 'em down too much," he snapped at her. "I don't want 'em tired."

"Sounds as if you're in no better mood than Midnight," she shot back.

He ignored that and went into the arena. She watched him unlatch the gate, swing it back and lead the colt through it, all with the slow, calm movements of a horseman, while his whole body screamed tension and fury. It was amazing how she could read him by now.

She turned back to the horse, checked the cinch one last time and went to see how Kristen was doing with the other one. She could hardly even see the girl or the horse, though, because she was still seeing Clint walking into the arena. And Clint looking at her with that flash of disdain in his eyes.

He would never change his opinion of her, no matter what. For her own sake, she needed to remember that. For everybody's sake.

She forced her mind onto inspecting Kristen's saddling job.

"Good work," she said. "You can go see Midnight now."

"Thanks, Cait."

Kristen ran toward the arena and Cait went back to the horse she'd saddled. She untied him and led him out toward Clint and Kristen.

Get used to it, she told herself. Get over it. Clint's

attracted to you—or he was—but he doesn't love you. Just stop loving him and there'll be no problem.

She wouldn't even let herself think about when *that* wish might come true.

But she could live with it. She'd lived with one-sided love all her life. If she could live with loving her parents when they didn't love her back, couldn't she do the same with Clint?

"Manuel!"

Startled, she glanced up to see Clint striding toward her, looking at something over her shoulder, his face dark as thunder. Behind him, Kristen had Midnight going around at the end of a longe line.

Cait looked back to see Manuel coming out of the tack room with an armload of dirty horse blankets. He looked as startled as she was.

"Get somebody in here to water this arena. I don't know what Joe's thinking letting it go so long."

Manuel looked at him for an instant, glanced at the dirt, then nodded.

"Right, boss. Anything else?"

"Not right now."

Manuel dumped the blankets into the back of the four-wheeler and went on about his business.

Clint closed the gate behind Cait before she could do it herself, slammed the latch into place and strode fast back toward Kristen and Midnight. The dust puffing up behind Midnight's hooves wasn't too bad. It hadn't been that long since the dirt had been sprinkled with the water wagon. Clint was just spoiling for a fight.

He spoke kindly enough to Kristen, though, and showed her how to urge Midnight to lope. Cait led the cutter out a little farther from the fence and mounted.

She blocked out everything else and focused on the horse. Riding was her refuge, had been since she was nine years old, and she gave herself to it gratefully. Staying as far as she could from the longeing activity in the other end of the arena, she rode the little gelding two-handed and tested to see how much he already knew and how supple he might be.

He began to get more and more comfortable with her and to realize that he couldn't take advantage of her, and she had just brought him into a lope for the first time when Clint's loud voice startled her again.

"What're you doing with this?"

It was an accusation, not a question, with an edge in his tone that got the attention of the horses, too. Her horse pricked his ears and looked toward Clint, while Midnight began loping more and more slowly, knowing that neither Clint nor Kristen noticed.

The two of them, big man and slender girl, stood facing each other, a few feet apart. Clint was holding something in his hand.

Cait's stomach clenched with sudden dread. She slowed her mount to a trot, then to a walk, got out of the circle she was making and started toward them.

"What is it?" Kristen's voice was high and clear.

"You know what it is. It was in your pocket."

Kristen lifted her hand to show him a tissue.

"This is what was in my pocket."

She put it to her nose and sneezed into it.

Then she said, "I didn't want to sneeze really loud and scare Midnight."

"Kristen," Clint said, and his voice rang hard as stone striking off the walls, "this concho was in your pocket. I picked it up from the dirt at your feet."

"Maybe it's been there a long time," she said calmly. "Maybe somebody lost it weeks ago."

She kicked at the soft ground of the arena.

"See?" she said. "It's really deep. It could've been covered and Midnight just turned it up."

Cait rode up to them and stopped.

Kristen turned to give her a beseeching look that tore at her heart. Cait knew just how she felt—she could almost see herself standing there with her aunt Maureen accusing her of some sin that had been committed by one of her hypocritical cousins.

"Cait…" Kristen said.

"Leave Cait out of this," Clint snapped. "Answer me. This came off my new saddle. It wasn't on the ranch weeks ago."

Kristen shrugged, glanced past him to the horse, tugged on the longe line and smooched to Midnight to get him going again. The colt obeyed her.

"How can you accuse me of stealing that off your saddle?" she demanded. "You are saying that I stole it, aren't you?"

"Now you're getting the picture," he drawled sarcastically.

"If it was in my pocket," she said, looking up at Clint sincerely, "somebody else must've put it there."

Clint's voice rose.

"Who? Me? Cait? Manuel? None of the other students have been here today."

Kristen's eyes widened. She was horrified.

"I'm not accusing y'all or any of my friends," she said firmly. "I don't know who did it."

There was a thread of desperation in her tone that twisted Cait's heart.

"Or when," Kristen added.

"It was on the saddle this morning," he snapped. "I rode the saddle. I noticed the concho was loose."

Kristen flashed a look at Cait that said she knew Cait would be against her, too.

It struck Cait to the bone. With her eyes, with the dip of her head, Kristen was saying she'd known all along she was bound to disappoint them.

"If it was loose," Kristen said, "maybe it fell off."

He glared at her.

"And into your pocket?" he said.

"It wasn't *in* my pocket," Kristen said.

"I saw it fall," Clint roared.

Stubbornly Kristen stood her ground, chin lifted, staring at him.

Exactly as Cait, herself, would've done at that

age. Kristen, too, had learned early that to survive she had to be tough.

"Clint, you're getting nowhere. She's told you she doesn't know anything about that concho."

"And I don't believe her."

"Because she's not from your world," Cait said flatly.

He flashed her a disgusted glance.

"It's true," she persisted hotly. "If Kristen's last name was Tolliver or Matheson or Kirkland or Carmack—if she came from one of the old Texas families who're invited to the Rocking M for Christmas Eve every year—you wouldn't be accusing her of stealing."

His disdain came back full force.

"I most certainly would—if she had my concho in her pocket."

Cait turned the disgust back on him.

"You're being completely unreasonable, and you know it."

"I'm not tolerating a thief on this ranch. I told you that from the get-go."

Kristen's face went paler than ever. Two spots of bright color sprang up along her cheekbones. Her eyes were bright with unshed tears.

Cait stood in the stirrup, threw her leg over and dismounted.

"Here," she said, thrusting the reins at Clint, "lope your own cutters.

"Come, Kristen," she said, "we need a trail ride.

Let Clint have Midnight and let's go get our horses.''

It would be the last trail ride either of them would ever take on the Rocking M, but Kristen didn't have to know that now.

Chapter Twelve

Cait was happy about one thing—she was back in touch with her old quick-decision survival skills. They had kicked in while Clint was standing there berating Kristen with such stubborn disbelief.

The truth had come to her in a blinding flash, just as it always had done: whether the girl had stolen something from him or not, Clint wasn't ever going to accept Kristen or any of the rest of these poor, drifting and troubled teenagers as rightfully belonging on his ranch, even temporarily. Therefore, he could never accept her, Cait, as belonging there permanently.

Not because she was their teacher or because she'd brought them there, but because she was a grown-up version of Kristen. Oh, he might be attracted to her and he might like to kiss her and he might have brought her to the Rocking M saying she should live there forever, but he'd had his reasons. He'd moved her here from Roy's to take care of her own horses, yes—and to entertain him. This hadn't been about her or her school. It had all been about Clint.

Bobbie Ann had said it, days ago. Clint needed all the distractions he could get.

He was the rock of this ranch, he was the one everybody came to with their problems, he was working 24/7. Clint had brought her here to entertain him, just as he'd said.

To Clint, she wasn't someone who really belonged on his ranch. She wasn't really a McMahan. Not permanently. She wasn't someone for him to love.

And she couldn't take any less.

That was the other truth she'd known in that moment there in the indoor arena sitting atop his cutting horse. Angry as she was with him at that moment when he was being so insensitive to Kristen, she'd loved him anyway. She had understood where he was coming from and *she had loved him anyway.*

Yes, she loved the security and the solidity of the ranch, and yes, she felt that both she and her school belonged here, but she loved Clint far, far more. She had loved John with all her heart, but she *loved* Clint. In a way she had never known existed. Her love for him was in her now, in her blood and her bones, and it always would be. She'd realized that at the same terrible moment she'd known that she must leave him.

No way could her battered heart bear the torture

of seeing him all the time and knowing the hard truth that he didn't love her back.

So, the same way she'd known what to do as a child when she'd sensed that her aunt was about to hit her, she had known what to do this afternoon. She had rescued Kristen from Clint, had gently tried to help the girl lower her expectations about Midnight, on the trail ride she had silently said goodbye to the ranch and now she was packing her bags.

For a moment she let her hands fall idle and just stood there beside her bed, staring out the wide east windows of her room. There was very little moonlight.

It was night, and she could slip away under cover of darkness.

But what an awful, cowardly way to go that would be! It went against every instinct she had, every facet of who she was.

But Bobbie Ann and her daughters had gone to Dallas on a shopping trip with Aunt Faylie and their friend Jo Lena, so she couldn't…didn't have to…tell them goodbye. She would leave them a letter. She would call them later and talk to them, or at least to Bobbie Ann.

Clint was the problem. He was here someplace— although she hadn't heard his boots on the stairs since she came up to her room hours ago—and she had to face him. For one thing, she wouldn't want him to think her a coward.

For another thing, she didn't want to think herself a coward.

Sudden tears poured from her eyes, stinging, rushing down her cheeks, and she turned her head so they wouldn't fall on her fancy boots she'd just placed in their boot bag. Dear Lord, she couldn't tell Clint goodbye in person.

She didn't even want to think about what she might do if she saw him, because her heart could betray her at any minute. It ached with love for him and it was so weighted down with the hopelessness of that love that she might blurt it all out to him as soon as she opened her mouth.

There were definite disadvantages to being an habitually direct, blunt person.

She'd be wanting to walk into his arms, she knew that for sure. She'd be longing to fall into another of those magical kisses with him so that the harsh, real world would vanish and she could feel the refuge in his arms.

Hardheaded and arrogant as he might be.

The tears fell harder now, and she broke into sobs. This wasn't like her, either. This wasn't like her at all.

Running into her bathroom, she fumbled with the tissue box, finally getting hold of one to wipe her face. It was soaked in a heartbeat.

Cait threw the soggy mess at the wastebasket, where it landed with a slightly satisfying plop. Then she turned on the cold water full blast and bent over the sink to bathe her face.

What in the *world?* Never did she lose control

like this. It was as if she'd turned into someone she didn't even know.

She could write Clint a note, too. There was no other way.

Yes, there was. She could go to a motel somewhere and try to sleep and by morning she'd have pulled herself together. Then she'd come back and talk to him.

But the instant she thought it, she knew the truth. Once she drove off the Rocking M, she could never bear to come back. She would send someone else to get her horses.

Holding a towel to her face with both hands, she went back into her bedroom to look at the clock. Eleven o'clock! Almost midnight! And she was still here.

This new person she'd turned into must have weights attached to her feet. Kristen had been gone since before dark and Manuel's crew had fed and watered her horses. She had absolutely no excuse for not being miles down the road by now.

However, she had no earthly clue as to which way she should go.

She sank onto the side of the bed, clenched her teeth and pulled the towel tight between her hands until the tears finally stopped. Then she sat up straight, put some steel in her spine and said a short prayer. Out loud, in a rough, cracked voice she didn't even recognize.

"Dear Lord. Help me get off this ranch. Give me the strength to load my truck, say goodbye to my horses and be gone from here. I love Clint too much to stay. God, please help me.''

As soon as Clint rode near enough to be seen from Jackson and Darcy's house, he switched the lantern from his right hand to his left and held it down on the off side of Midnight. They'd still see a light moving if they looked out, though, so he'd just have to hope that they were too interested in each other to be gazing out the windows.

It'd be too much of a shock for them. It'd be startling enough for him to be seen going into the chapel in the daytime, much less making a lantern-lit ride to it in the middle of the night. But he didn't know where else to go. He was miserable, he was about to explode from the riot of feelings inside him, he was on the edge of losing his mind and his judgment.

He was riding a green two-year-old through the dark, wasn't he? And as if that weren't suicidal enough, he was hallucinating that he might have fallen in love with Cait.

Why else—why else, dear God, would I be so torn up about her wanting me to be John?

Maybe God would answer that question if Clint prayed it in the chapel. And this one, too.

Why else, dear God, would I be thinking that she's going to leave here? Why would I be thinking that, when those are words she didn't even say?

With his mind in such a fit, he didn't know how he kept his body relaxed and easy in the saddle and

the pace a slow trot, but he did. It would never do
to let Midnight feel tension in him, because the colt
might get all worked up, too.

Even more of a shock to Jackson and Darcy than
seeing Clint go into the chapel would be having him
get thrown into their yard at midnight by a rank colt
who should be in the barn. Midnight seemed to love
this, though. The new experiences stirred his curiosity and the exercise calmed him and he was looking around and smelling the air so much he seemed
to have forgotten Clint was on his back.

So far, so good. They rode past Jackson's house.

Images of the Nighthorse in Kristen's song kept
drifting into Clint's head and he kept trying to shut
them out. There was no big moon tonight, and no
mountains from which to fly into the sky. And no
shy, innocent girl to make friends with this horse.

She had betrayed his friendship by stealing from
him! He would never have guessed that, and the
knowledge stung him. Her trust had gentled this colt
immeasurably, yet no one could trust her.

Clint glanced back at Jackson's silent house and
hung the lantern from the saddle horn again. At least
he was outside and moving. He might be in danger
of being thrown into the next county, but he couldn't
have paced the barn aisle one more minute, and he
certainly couldn't have gone to the house with Cait
there.

"Cait."

Midnight pricked his ears and turned them back
to listen for more.

"I'm not talking to you," Clint said.

He was in deep trouble if he couldn't resist simply saying her name.

Major trouble. Because she certainly could resist saying his.

She could even kiss him as if she meant it and then say John's name instead.

That awful moment sliced his heart through again, with its sharp cruelty as fresh as the first time.

He had to get this straight in his head and then nail it down in his stubborn, stupid heart—in spite of what he, Clint, had thought all these months, Cait *had* loved John. In the past two or three weeks she had made friends with Clint, she had flirted with Clint, she had kissed Clint, but all of that was only using him as a substitute for John.

It figured. Not one woman he'd ever dated had loved him for himself. Always, always, they'd had a hidden or not-so-hidden agenda. Cait's was a little different, that was all.

His gut twisted.

Oh, yes, Cait was different. She was the only one he had ever loved.

That figured, too. Since she was the only one he could never have.

"Way to go, McMahan."

His horse muttered deep in his throat.

"Get used to it," Clint said to him. "I'll talk to myself if I want to."

Cait's loyalty wasn't to him, either. Even if she didn't love him, she could show a little loyalty.

She'd stood right there and defended Kristen when anybody with a grain of sense knew the girl had to have stolen that piece of silver.

And when she'd handed him the reins of his cutter and told him to ride him himself, she'd spoken in such a flat, final tone that it had chilled his bones and made him fighting mad, all at the same time. He ought to tell her to take her thieving teenagers and get off the ranch. He really should. For the good of the ranch.

But that tone in her voice had beaten him to it. The tone and the words. *Lope your own cutters.* That was a job she'd agreed to do, and she was quitting it.

She was leaving here, he knew, and doing it because he'd tried to stop Kristen from stealing. Couldn't Cait see that it was for the good of the girl?

His jaw hardened. Kristen was a real disappointment to him. He'd have sworn she had more moral fiber than that.

But he didn't intend to care about Kristen. He didn't care about any of those silly kids.

He picked up the lantern again and held it out to light the way through a darker stretch where the faint moonlight didn't reach at all. Then Midnight sped up to climb the little rise up to the graveled road that led from the highway to Jackson's house.

The chapel sat on the other side of that narrow road and he could vaguely see its shape in the darkness. The cross on top showed clearly, though. The moonlight seemed to gather in it and make it gleam white in the night.

It drew him to it.

He would go in there and pray that he wouldn't love Cait. He would pray for good sense and to see the reality that Cait loved John. All she knew or felt about Clint was that he *wasn't* John.

As he looked down again, something caught his eye, something moving on the ground between him and the chapel. Midnight threw up his head and nickered. The something nickered back.

The other horse ambled toward them and climbed up onto the road. Clint stared in disbelief.

"Daisy! Is that you?"

It was. And, as usual, she wasn't going to let him get close enough to catch her. As Clint came nearer, she left the road and angled off it, only mildly interested in the fact that she now had company.

His cell phone was in his hand before he even knew he'd reached to take it from the holder on his belt, the number punched in before he thought.

"Cait?"

"Clint?"

She sounded surprised. And breathless. He listened to the sound of his name, still lingering in his ear. Did she sound pleased, too? Maybe just a little bit happy to hear his voice?

He jerked himself up short. So what? Who cared if Cait was pleased? She certainly didn't care anything about *his* feelings.

"Your mare is out again," he said. "And I'm not

gonna spend the rest of the night trying to catch her.''

"*Daisy?*"

"Right."

"How'd she get out with that safety latch on?"

"Maybe somebody left it undone," he said. "Did you check it yourself?"

"I haven't been to the barn since Manuel's crew did my chores."

"One of 'em hasn't learned how the latch works, then."

"Where are you?" Cait said.

You. Not *Daisy.*

A thrill touched Clint's blood. Which only went to prove how pathetic he was. He had to get a grip on his feelings. He wasn't going to let himself love her, he was *not*.

"Over by the chapel," he said.

"You've been chasing her? Oh, Clint, I'm sorry. I'll be right there."

I'll be right there.

Again, that quick happiness in his blood. *Insanity.* She wasn't coming to him. She was coming to get her mare.

"Bring a halter," he said.

"Right."

Then she was gone.

Slowly Clint closed his phone and replaced it on his belt. Why had he done that? Why had he called her?

Cait was the last person in the world he needed to see.

Cait was the *only* person in the world he *wanted* to see.

He rode up into the chapel yard and leaned over to set the lantern on the low wall that fanned out from the low steps of the approach to the door. Then he sat his horse for a minute, slowly taking the coil of rope from his saddle. He slid it onto his shoulder as he rode at a walk toward a patch of grass where he stopped Midnight and stepped down, taking the set of soft hobbles from his pocket as soon as he hit the ground.

He slipped the hobbles around the colt's forelegs and tied up his reins. As he'd expected, Daisy came up to greet them, carefully staying out of his reach.

"Life's tough," he told her, and threw out the loop of his rope as he turned.

It fell neatly over her head. She came to him sweetly before he even tugged on the rope, stood patiently while he fashioned a hackamore and put it on her head, then followed like a puppy as he led her to the big mesquite tree and tied her.

"Daisy, you're all bluff," he said.

Then he crossed the short distance to the wall and picked up the lantern to show him the way into the chapel. He had to have some divine help before Cait arrived. God help him, he wasn't going to let himself love her.

He was *not*.

* * *

Cait pulled to the side of the road in front of the chapel and turned off the motor. The sound of it stopped, and so did the weak spin of her churning stomach. For an instant. Only until it gathered itself and spiraled up again, stronger than ever.

She started to hit the headlight switch, then she stopped.

Could she really be seeing what she thought she was seeing?

Daisy. Yes, Daisy. Securely tied to a tree.

Clint hadn't needed her to come catch this mare!

Something moved to her left. She caught it in the corner of her eye, and lost her breath. Clint?

No. The faint moonlight showed her the shape of a saddled horse, hobbled, grazing.

She stared, then rolled her window down so the sight would be unobstructed.

Midnight. The tall, rangy colt was unmistakable in profile.

Clint had ridden *Midnight* all the way over here in the *dark?*

The doors to the chapel stood open. Deep inside it, a soft yellow light glowed.

The weakness in her stomach spread to her legs and her knees knocked together. She managed to hit the light switch before she grabbed the steering wheel to try to steady herself.

Dear God, You mean for me to talk to him now.

It wasn't even a question, because she knew. This was God's plan.

She leaned her forehead against the steering

wheel while the knowledge settled into the pit of her stomach. There wouldn't be any waiting until tomorrow. She had to pull herself together tonight.

Finally she straightened and looked out the window again.

The chapel doors were standing open and a light shone inside. Clint.

Her heart was pounding so hard she thought she could hear it. Clint. Clint.

Clint.

He was inside the chapel, waiting for her. He was bound to have heard her drive up.

Still she sat, for a long time, looking at the light. What would he say to her? What would she say to him?

Finally she turned and reached for the halter on the seat beside her. But her hands were shaking so that she couldn't bear to look at them and she let it fall, buckles clattering, onto the floorboard. She couldn't let Clint see her shaking like this!

But suddenly she couldn't bear to sit there anymore, either, so she opened the door, got out, quietly closed it and leaned back against it, crossing her arms beneath her breasts to still them. After a long moment, she stepped forward.

Help me, Lord. Give me the words, the right words. If I say any wrong ones, don't let him hear them. Please, dear God, let him hear only the right words from me.

Slowly, but without any more hesitation, she

walked up the dark path and past the low adobe wall toward the light inside the chapel.

When she reached the doorway, Clint was sitting sideways on one of the long oak benches at the front, his arm along the back of it, his eyes on the door. He stood up, facing her, with the lantern behind him on the old plain altar.

"Cait."

There was such a weight of emotion in his voice, so many different feelings that she couldn't sort out, much less put a name to, that she stopped and just stood there for a minute. They eyed each other warily.

A sudden desperation rose in her breast. This was it. Her last chance. Her only chance.

"I'm sorry Daisy's put you to such trouble," she said, and started walking down the aisle toward him. "How'd you come to go to my barn and find her gone, anyway?"

"I didn't. I was riding over here and came across her."

She stared at him.

"You were out on a night ride?"

"I couldn't sit down, much less sleep."

"Why not?"

"You're leaving."

Shock rippled through her. Her knees were still weak, but she kept walking anyway. Toward him. Toward Clint.

"Why'd you say that?"

"I knew it. By your tone of voice when you quit your job for me."

Another shock, made stronger by a quick elation, surged in her blood. He hadn't been able to sleep because of her—because of her leaving.

But more than that, her heart cried, *he read me right.* He had known her unspoken intentions!

"I can't believe you knew me that well. Clint."

She'd had to feel his name on her tongue. She needed to say it again.

"Believe it. Cait."

She walked up to him and they stood looking at each other in the soft lamplight.

"What I should've believed was what you said to Kristen," she said. "She did take that concho off your new saddle."

A brief, sharp hurt showed in his eyes. He turned away, as if to hide it, and sat down heavily in the same place again. She sat, too, on that front bench, an arm's length away, sitting sideways to face him.

"I'm so sorry," Cait said. "I should've had more sense than to think she was innocent, but at least my believing her put more pressure on her conscience and she confessed during our trail ride."

He made a dismissive gesture, then faced the altar fully and dropped his head into his hands.

Cait laid her arm along the top of the bench, aching to reach out to him.

"I don't care," he muttered. "I just expected more from her, that's all, after we arranged to let her work with Midnight and…"

He looked and sounded so miserable that Cait interrupted.

"She didn't want to take it, Clint," she said, "but it had the Rocking M brand on it and she was desperate for a souvenir of the ranch—she says she's happier here than anyplace she's ever been."

He lifted his head and flashed a glance that was mostly incredulous, but there was deeper pain in it, too.

"Kristen's never in one place longer than a month or two, Clint. Her aunt could decide to move on tonight."

He shook his head helplessly.

"I would've *given* her something with the brand on it. A dozen things. Even the concho. I could've had another one made. All she had to do was ask."

Her gaze held his, willing him to hear her.

"Why would she ask? Why would she even think about asking? No one's ever *given* Kristen anything, Clint. This school, this ranch, is her first experience with people who believe in the Lord and give out of the goodness of their hearts."

He thought about that and nodded. Then he shrugged, as if to be rid of the whole subject.

"Kristen wrote you a note of apology and left it on your desk in the office."

"I don't care," he said again.

"You don't want to care," Cait told him, "but you do. It's okay, Clint. We're all human, whether we want to be or not."

"Oh?" he said bitterly as he whirled on the seat

to face her fully. "Is that why you kissed me and then told me I'm not John? Because you're only human?"

He clamped his mouth shut so fast she knew he wished he'd never said it. But his gray eyes on hers had a quick, hard storm springing to life in them, raging for an answer.

Cait got a lump in her throat.

"You didn't let me finish that sentence that day," she said. "I was trying to say that John had loved me unconditionally, but that you never could because you'll always blame me for his death."

His intense eyes narrowed and he searched her face for ages, trying to see whether that was the truth.

"So you were thinking about whether I loved you or not?"

"Yes."

"Because you love the ranch so much?"

She held his gaze and shook her head, sighing.

"I'm not like all the other women, Clint. If I were, I would never have moved back to Roy's after John died. Think about it."

He turned his head away, then looked at her again.

"I don't still blame you for John's death," he said quietly. "I started praying about that right after Christmas."

"Why?"

"Because it wasn't fair. Nobody can say what would've happened if you'd gone with him to Mexico. Knowing you, and how bold you are, you would've refused to stay in town and he might have gone anyway. You might have both been killed in the desert.''

He laid his arm along the top of the bench and touched the tips of her fingers with his.

"Forget I ever said that, okay, Cait? I'm sorry." She nodded.

They looked into each other's eyes for two long heartbeats.

"But you'll always love John," he said quietly.

"Yes. I will always love his memory. John treated me better than any man I had ever met and he loved me with no reservations and brought me to my faith in God. Loving him changed me from an uncertain girl into a woman who knows her own mind."

That made him grin a little.

"Hard to imagine," he said. "An uncertain Cait."

"I tried to hide it," she said, grinning back.

He sobered quickly and his gray eyes pierced hers again.

"So what does your woman's mind tell you now?"

"That I did love John, but that I *love* you," she said simply, and was surprised at how easy that was to say, at how much she needed to say it. "I love you, Clint."

He searched her face as if he wanted to see those words written on her skin. Then he steadied her trembling arm with his strong fingers as if she couldn't talk anymore without that support. It did give her courage. She took a deep breath.

"Clint," she said quietly, "if I've learned anything from working with these kids, and from growing up as that kind of kid myself, it's that God doesn't limit love. Loving one person only increases our capacity for loving another person."

They kept on looking at each other. Neither of them moved. His fingers warmed her through her sleeve.

"If you don't love me, I'll still love you," she said, holding his gaze with hers, amazed that she could say those words without her lips going stiff with tears. "I'll go someplace else and I'll set up my school and I'll work at my job and I'll build my career. But I will always love you."

He lifted his hand and moved closer to her, reaching to smooth back a curl from her face. Then he tucked it behind her ear with an infinitely tender touch.

She would never, ever forget that touch.

Then her heart rocketed in her chest as he leaned forward and kissed her. Very, very gently he brushed her lips with his. Once, then again.

He drew back a little, to look into her eyes, but he put his hand on her shoulder and softly caressed her neck. Then he stood up and reached for her hand.

"Come with me," he said, his voice low and compelling. "Come outside and look at the sky."

They walked hand in hand up the aisle and out

through the wide doors onto the steps. The wind was rising. The darkness closed around them. For a long moment they stood there, listening to the trees move, watching the night and the darker shapes of the horses.

"The Rocking M," he said. "I love this land."

"So do I," Cait said, her face to the wind. "It even smells better than other places."

Clint turned to her and lifted his hands to her face, brushed back her hair and looked down into her eyes. There was just enough light from the lantern inside to see his expression.

"I love this land," he said again, "but I would leave it to be with you if that's what you wanted, Cait. I love you more."

"I know you do. Otherwise, you'd never have known I was leaving."

"Are you staying now?"

She smiled.

"That depends on what you say next."

"Will you marry me, Cait McMahan?"

She took his face in both her hands.

"I will," she said, "Clint McMahan."

He pulled back, out of her hands, but his eyes never left hers as he reached into the front pocket of his jeans.

"Well, then, since I'll have you with me," he said, "I guess I won't need this anymore."

"What? What is it?"

He showed her. The mustard-seed necklace John

had given her lay, gleaming and tiny, in the palm of his big hand.

Tears sprang to her eyes. She stroked it with one finger, and the warmth of his body moved through it to hers.

"Clint! You found it?"

"Yes. And, coward that I was, I kept it so I'd have something of yours…"

He swallowed hard.

"If you left again."

Cait couldn't even speak—she could only look at him and look at him some more. He had already convinced her, but now she had proof twofold. He loved her. He truly did love her.

"You're right," she whispered, caressing him with her eyes. "You won't need it anymore."

He pulled her to him, she threw her arms around his neck and suddenly he was kissing her with all his heart.

She kissed him back the very same way.

* * * * *

Prodigal son Monte returns home
to the Rocking M to heal his body,
his soul—and his heart, in

LONG WAY HOME,

book three of

THE McMAHANS OF TEXAS.

Available February 2003, only from
Steeple Hill Love Inspired.

Dear Reader,

This story of the oldest McMahan brother, Clint, and Cait McMahan, who is his widowed sister-in-law, is one that touches my heart. At some time in all our lives we reach a midnight hour that tests our trust and makes us reach for our faith, even if it seems as small as a mustard seed.

From the moment Cait comes back to the Rocking M Ranch with her newly bought horses and her heartfelt plans to establish a horsemanship school for troubled teenagers, Clint is trying to find a way to trust her and the feelings between them—as well as to trust God to direct the decisions that he always feels are his responsibility alone.

While you are reading Clint and Cait's story, I'm writing about Clint and Jackson's brother, Monte, who finally comes home after six long years of barely communicating with the family. I hope you will look for his story, *Long Way Home*, coming in February 2003.

Please let me know how you like this book. I would love to hear from you. You can reach me c/o Steeple Hill Books, 300 East 42nd Street, New York, NY 10017.

All best wishes,

Gena Dalton